THE MYSTERIOUS MR HARRINGTON

JAMIE JENNINGS

THE MYSTERIOUS MR HARRINGTON

First edition. April 14, 2022.

E-book ISBN: 978-0-6452408-4-9
Paperback ISBN: 978-0-6452408-3-2

Copyright © 2022 Jamie Jennings.

Written by Jamie Jennings.
Cover Illustration: Kang Dee
Editor: Hoffman Smith

NOTE: NSFW

This book contains scenes of an explicit sexual nature.

CHAPTER ONE

His moans had rapidly increased in pace and loudness as he aggressively jerked himself to his personal pleasures. Finally, he erupted all of his warm load into the bathroom sink as he watched his almost 11-inch shaft throb rhythmically between his legs before he let go. Looking into the mirror, he felt more saddened about himself, his sexuality, and his general self–esteem because it seemed like not even a single soul was in line with getting sexual with him, not even his ex-boyfriend, who had initially thought he could shake Fletcher's huge size, and it was not long before they both realized that he was wrong!

Fletcher Harrington was on the rather very handsome and appealing side and general physique; his eyes were glossy blue, beautiful blonde hair, an impressive, slightly athletic build, and basically sexually appealing to the average human being. He lived with his mother, Janet, in a small town on the Alabama Gulf Coast before he resumed senior year. And his mother, on the other hand, knew the kinds of apparent pains he'd been having to go through because of his sexuality and general personality. She had a problem with him spending almost all of his time in his bedroom without socializing or doing any other "normal" thing with other people. And she always knew that he'd been masturbating and pleasing himself too, but she'd appeared rather very powerless most of the time.

He had royal heritage in his bloodline! His father, was a royal monarch in power in Switzerland. But his mother had always gone against his father's political ventures and was not keen on having her only son go down his father's "ugly path". But he was his father's only son and had two younger sisters that he'd hardly ever talked to! At the same time, he and his mother had always endeavored to stay away from the public image while in the United States, making sure that absolutely no one got to find out about who he really was! But he was comfortable with it too; he took his introverted genes from his mother, conspicuously, and never wanted to have anything to do with public topics either—his mother's son.

Fletcher was a chronic masturbator, and from a young age as well, but always considered himself a virgin because he hadn't experienced what the insides of a male, female or any sensual figure at all had truly ever felt like! As a teenager, he'd always got horny really easily and was always sad about not being able to get laid by people he was involved with. The last person he tried to penetrate was Daniel. An old friend had forced him to come with him to a party once. They had gotten tipsy from the excessive alcohol they'd had that night, and they could tell that they had been extremely horny too, and when they had decided to lay off some steam, they get to realize that it wasn't possible because Daniel was too tight, and Fletcher was just too big!

It had started off slowly in the backseat of Daniel's car. After they had made out with each other like their lives depended on it for some minutes, then Daniel rejecting Fletcher's kind request for a blowjob before getting down totally, big mistake. And when he flipped Daniel over to thrust his already warm and juicy booty hole, he watched Daniel spread his booty cheeks right in front of him and pull him closer. Fletcher aggressively pushed his hard shaft into him, and when he screamed, it was loud enough to wake the dead! And just like the others, Fletcher hadn't been able to go past Daniel's entrance! Daniel pushed Fletcher out of him immediately and gave him a hard slap on the face!

"What the fuck, Fletcher? What did you put in me!?", he exclaimed in utter shock!

Fletcher was non-responsive to the question as he was already used to such reactions to him and the behemoth between his legs. There was nothing else he could do than to apologize to Daniel. They had never talked since then. Daniel had been a kind person to Fletcher all the while, and when it was time for them to express some of that emotion to each other, his huge size put him in a helpless mess, again.

Throughout almost all of his teenage years, the size of his shaft had remained a major disaster to his mental and sexual health for a longer time than anyone could have ever imagined, and he rarely talked about it to anyone, not even his mother, this had been slowly building a subtly underlying mental resistance toward the opposite gender, in his mind! It seemed like the masturbation had already slowly been getting the best of him, and he was most comfortable with it even sooner than he'd thought and never made any sexual advances to anyone anymore because he almost always knew how it was going to turn out to be!

Even now that he was in senior year, he was always scared to have to involve himself in anything that required him to penetrate the other folk! He had gotten rather very comfortable with his masturbation comfort, and he was ready to carry on with it for a very long time as well!

He'd always tried to mix up with his new friends, male and female, and regularly struggled to get along with anyone, especially Jayden, a bully by nature, also a well physically built folk, who subconsciously decided to keep proving to Fletcher that he could be the only "strongest" guy in the class then! As stupid as it had sounded, Fletcher always decided to let everything slide until it got to the point where Fletcher lost his cool on him and quickly handed Jayden's butt back to him, right in the presence of a senior educator, in the middle of a teaching session! An action that led him to the principal's office for disciplinary actions! His mother was also invited for the visit!

Time for the "disciplinary appointment" came by eventually and Fletcher was more nervous than he had initially been. Seeming more introverted and timid than he had been when he was even 16. He had never been pulled into the principal's office before and blamed Jayden for getting him into such a mess because if everyone had respected themselves, there would have been no reason for his mom to get invited by Principal Elliot for his insubordination! He didn't even know how to look at his mom or properly carry himself most times, but he tried to all the same.

On walking into the space, as cold as his spine had been, he could notice that principal Elliot's office space was completely "state-of-the-art" enough, and his mom was somewhat bothered about what she might have to do or say to save her son from any strict punishments under such a coordinated-looking facility! But she was willing, nonetheless, basically the best mom she could be for her only son. So his mother had him sit at the waiting spot for a while, so she could meet up with principal Elliot first to talk briefly and maybe, ask some questions too, and then when she had gotten as much "understanding" as she could, she then went in asking Fletcher to go in with her. His primal essence quickly notices that Principal Elliot is as sexy as anything! His body effortlessly filled up his dress shirt and the entire outfit. Hispecs were literally outspoken and captivating enough to make a Pope look twice. His silky red hair flowed down his shoulders, a bit in front and a bit behind him. His emerald green eyes fired impulsive gazes through his rectangular, matte black-framed glasses. Although he looked like he was in his mid-forties already, he was a beautiful one! And Fletcher was awed! It was the first time he had witnessed the new principal so up close!

Fletcher watched his mother and the principal briefly exchange whatever they were or had been talking about and decided that he was going to say absolutely nothing until he was allowed or requested to speak! And that was exactly what he did! He heard the principal tell his mom that he had known everything he wanted and that it was time for him to have alone time with Fletcher to better understand his own perspectives! She concurred and then walked slowly to her son, gave him a soft pat on his right shoulder, and told him that he was going to be just fine, assuring that she trusted him so much still!

The door of his office opened and was shut tightly again. Principal Elliot walked past Fletcher to ensure that the door was properly locked and then slowly walked towards Fletcher, realizing just how young, obviously teenage, worried-looking, handsome, muscular dude of a guy Fletcher was. Elliot quickly requests that Fletcher sit down on the chair opposite him and goes in for a conversation about the situation on the ground; reasons why he engaged Jayden in a fight. Fletcher easily found himself explaining to Elliot about everything that had really happened, about how he had been getting painfully picked on by Jayden for a long time now, and how his reaction in the class had only built up frustrations over time towards Jayden! In no time, he realized that he had been finding it easy to talk to him eventually, contrary to what he thought would be the case when he got there at first. Even for a man at his age, probably mid-thirties, he still noticed the bouncy, juicy-looking pecs in front of him, staring at him in the face; he found himself getting easily aroused by the way he looked at Elliot, the way he talked back to him in such a calm manner, with a conspicuous sweet tone, the way he gently moved his body from left to right, repeating the cycle as he listened to him talk as well.

Eventually, he lost focus on what Principal Elliot was saying to him and started paying more aggressive attention to his "assets". For reasons he couldn't understand or fathom, he couldn't seem to resist what he was seeing right there. The principal was oozing sexual energy, and he couldn't help it. He had an 11inch erection, so even if he actually had the chance to do anything with this sexy man staring at him, he might chicken out too, so he thought, even though he knew that was likely impossible at that time, his cravings got the best of him still, and his erection was visible enough to principal Elliot. One that got him surprised and easily delighted at the same time!

After the now-boring session he had been having with Principal Elliot, he snapped back from his fantasies when the school official asked him to go over to the other desk at the far side of the office space, an empty desk, and wait for Elliot there. He did. And after scribbling his pen on some paperwork that had been scattered all over his desk, Elliot walked over to where Fletcher had been impatiently seated and waiting for him, then asked him to lie comfortably on his back, pulled his jean pants and underwear, to reveal Fletcher's already throbbing and hungry erection.

"But, Sir!" Fletcher said out loudly in utter shock over what was happening right there!

"Shhhhhh! Oh my! That's a big one!" he whispered in wholesome surprise over the size of this teenager, as his large veins on his erection pulsed in his palm!

Eventually, in no time, he watched the principal aggressively jerk him off while explaining to Fletcher about the "sensitive spots" on his shaft that Elliot was noticing, and still kept jerking Fletcher's erection as Fletcher started to moan uncontrollably while trying so hard to remain silent so as not to attract any unwanted attention. Fletcher was having the moment of his life right there and didn't want anything or anyone ruining it for him!

The principal struggled to keep himself together as this warm throbbing erection in front of him looked like it needed some swallowing from him too! Elliot was easily tempted to go beyond jerking Fletcher and sink his lips down this thick shaft and lick its tip too. But he remained mostly on the rather "professional" side; he probably wasn't sure about how his student was going to react if he eventually gave him a blowjob right there and maybe ride on him and have him spill his warm cum into him afterward. Elliot knew his own erection was soaking up his jockstrap already. Fletcher's size was the most impressive he had seen in a while, and he knew how much he really wanted to have a taste and feel of it, but he couldn't at that point, and it was disappointing enough for him.

Elliot stuck with jerking Fletcher, and as Fletcher's moans got louder, his paces got faster; he knew he was about to climax; Elliot also wanted to have a feel of that hot semen all over his hands. Right there, he had developed a fetish for Fletcher and his size already, and that wasn't a problem for him. Fletcher watched in complete ecstasy as Elliot jerked him with all his attention and "professionalism" because he seemed really, really good at it. It left Fletcher wondering if all this intense pleasure had been the "punishment" he was up for all the while, or if it was a set-up of some sorts, but he didn't mind; he was caught up in the moment!

Fletcher climaxed in no time! It was an aggressive one! Shooting warm liquid into the air as his ejaculations came through, he moaned out like never before! He got some on the empty desk there, some on his jean pants and the last of the heated fluid on Principal Elliot's hands.

"Tell me how much you loved that; how do you feel, Fletcher?"

"Oh my god! Never better! I feel great, Sir, what was that?!" he exclaimed as he struggled slightly to catch his breath.

"Good, now you're going to listen carefully! No one, absolutely no one should get to know about this, not even your mom, or anyone else at all, understood?!" He warned in a slightly aggressive tone!

"Yes, yes Sir, zipped! He responded with aggressive head-nodding gestures in reflex response to his warnings!

"Right, I know with this size of yours, you have been struggling to get laid by your peers, still a virgin, or am I wrong?" he asked bluntly!

"Yes, yes Sir, that too!" he responded hurriedly, as uncertainty clouded the atmosphere around him there!

"Good, now you're going to lick me like your life depends on it, and as time goes on, you get to feel more of this body and get laid, just you and I! What do you think?!" he said to him in sensual tone!

A statement that awakened his shaft again and heightened his libido effortlessly! He nodded his head again and then watched Principal Elliot come over to where he was, and position his big round booty on his face, and had him bless his booty hole with Fletcher's warm tongue and lips, kissing his opening vigorously as he couldn't help but moan out loudly in utmost delight! Fletcher had been so good that Elliot found himself shaking to his tunes in no time, his orgasm threshold was exhausted immediately, and his slight scream and smooth, vibrating thighs confirmed that he had just reached peak pleasure effortlessly!

And when Fletcher was now able to at least get up from the table, he jumped into his pants and thanked the principal profoundly! Explaining to him that no one had ever made him feel as good as that, and he wanted more of it if he didn't mind!

It was the first time he'd been jerked off like that, with so much "experience", so it seemed! It was the first time he'd had such an intense orgasm, he'd never shoot sperm out of his cock like that before, and now, all thanks to the principal's apparent "professionalism", it was granted, and this was probably going to be the start of something beautiful with him, or anyone else, or so he'd thought.

His mom had been waiting for him outside in the school car park, and she had been expecting to drive him back home after she'd understood the kind of punishment he was going to experience from the school authority!

It was a few people left in the building now, Principal Elliot and Fletcher slowly walked past the classrooms and then out towards the car park, en route to his car, so he could drive him over to his place to finish what they started! When they stumbled on his mom, Elliot explained that he needed to have Fletcher come over to his place to pick up some precise materials for his rehabilitation. Mrs. Harrington concurred and let Fletcher go with Principal Elliot and pleaded with Fletcher to not get into any forms of trouble again this time, requesting that he return home as soon as he could. Fletcher acknowledged and hurried into the principal's SUV, as impatient as he was to have his libido graced!

It was a short 30-mile drive back home, and Elliot watched as his student looked and seemed less depressed than he had appeared earlier on. He had asked Fletcher how he felt about the whole "encounter", if he approved of his methods, if he was okay, so far, if he'd really felt better about it, or remorse. Fletcher agreed that it was all on a positive note and told his principal that he was really looking forward to continuing what they had started at the office! Even though he had been exhausted from a seemingly long day, still assuring him that he'd never felt that good in a very long time! Even though the principal had personal issues of his own, with men always taking him for granted because he was too busy with his career and never wanted to get into anything serious with him, coupled with the fact that they hadn't sported a "cock" his size! Elliot knew he was in for a great time, all the way! He couldn't wait to have all that huge goodness inside of him, scrapping his slippery walls and filling him up completely!

And when they had gotten to his place, the cozy space of his principal's residence was quickly captivating enough! Fletcher could tell effortlessly as he was directed to a bedroom to relax his head and get more comfortable while Elliot went to fix some other things!

A few moments later, he returned and had found Fletcher shirtless, sleeping deeply on the bed there already! Elliot slowly shut the door behind him as he advanced towards him, where he'd laid. Fletcher's athletic build easily aroused him more intensely this time. The first thing he did was lean into his torso area, caressing his strong abs with his soft hands and slowly reaching for his underpants.

"Oh my, good God!" he'd exclaimed to himself as he felt his flaccid girth with his palm. It had still been too good and huge to be true! It was warm, thick, and felt "capable", the most capable he had ever come across all his life. He was turned on instantly, beyond his control. He swiftly pulled off his underpants and unloaded his humongous size, waking him up in the process.

"Heyyy it's okay, darling, it's me, Elliot, I'm helping you out with a little more sensuality now, relax, okay?" he said to him calmly.

"Oh, okay sir, but I dunno, are we..." Fletcher gently muttered before Elliot placed his finger on his lips and softly asked him to enjoy the entire moment instead. He too, was already stimulated by the sight of him holding his shaft the way he did. And when he started jerking him off again, his moans easily told him how he had felt about it. Elliot stroked Fletcher's warm rod nicely, flipping his palms from top to bottom; it seemed like that was just the way he loved it, like the last time. Elliot was always blown away by his size and couldn't have enough of it; he always wanted to feel and grace it with his hands, with every opportunity he had gotten!

He was easily reminded of how good Fletcher was with his shaft at his office during the school period, but this time, it wasn't in the office or at any official premises; it was in his house, in his personal bedroom! And as much as he already wanted to sink his throbbing erection into any hole he could find there, his intuition stopped the thoughts instantly; he believed there was no way he was ever going to see himself getting down with Fletcher, it seemed like it was just all fantasies! He was wrong.

He kept with the rather very gentle stroking on Fletcher's shaft and maintained the pace; Elliot knew he was going to have sex with Fletcher eventually, at that point. His jockstrap was drenched in the hot juices pumping out of his wet, hungry erection and booty hole already and it had to be graced by Fletcher's warm thick cock. He wasn't scared of the size either, he had been hunting for a guy Fletcher's size all his life, and apparently, he'd found it, he was going to seize the moment! A still slightly uncertain Fletcher tried to "respectfully" bail when he figured things had been going "out of hand", but he realized it was real and hardcore when Elliot took off his shirt completely, exposing his rather very juicy, bouncy pecs to him.

"Alright little one, come have some of that," Elliot said softly as he watched Fletcherplace his thick throbbing erection in-between Elliot's pair of warm lips. Fletcher was adamant about it at first, and he could easily understand why, but he was horny to the teeth already; he was hornier, it had to be done!

So right there, Elliot eases some of Fletcher's tension, first asking if Fletcher was okay with him touching him and maybe, kissing him too, indifferent at first, for a brief moment, but Fletcher concurred, eventually, giving in to his primal instincts, in the end. Looking at him there, he kept on getting reminded of how much of a rather very beautiful man principal Elliot was;

even at his age, he was more beautiful and sexually appealing to Fletcher than most of his high school crushes ever have been. Fletcher knew he had to completely free himself to actually enjoy the sexual moment and ease himself off any pressures. So he allowed the tension to drop, and he could find himself getting even more aroused and his warm shaft getting even harder in no time, just by staring at Elliot's beautiful face and the bouncy, juicy, succulent pecs!

After a short moment of looking into each other's eyes, in sheer awkwardness, Principal Elliot then decides to take things slowly and sensually with Fletcher instead of rushing it. He leaned in and moved his neck forward, softly brushing his lower lip with Fletcher's before pausing to look at him again. Fletcher kissed him back. Elliot quickly realized that Fletcher was even a GOOD kisser. They stop to look at each other for a moment again; right there, they felt some awkward spark and mutual desire between them!

Fletcher pulled Elliot back to kiss him again, expecting it to be even better than it was previously; this time, things got a little bit more intense; they got aggressive more quickly than they could have imagined! Fletcher pulled off his soft lips from Elliot's. He went straight to Elliot's neck like he was wired to do it! Elliot now loved the feeling! Elliot easily forgot that Fletcher was his school student, and Fletcher easily forgot that Elliot was his principal too! Fletcher started to moan out lightly as his tongue found its way across the areas of Elliot's neck that drove him crazy, so crazy that Elliot had started to moan a little bit louder than he had been! Elliot was shocked by Fletcher's effortless ability to make him feel the way he did! It was not by mere chance that Fletcher was this good; he must have been consuming some serious porn content too, he thought to himself. Fletcher slowly reached for Elliot's warm, sexy-looking muscles and gently made his way to his pecs and started to massage them rather passionately, to his principal's utmost surprise!

"How do you like that, Sir?", Fletcher asked gently.

Elliot nodded his head in an awkwardly speechless response. He was calm and horny beyond his imagination now and couldn't wait for his hungry booty hole to eat up Fletcher's huge and apparently hungry erection.

Elliot gently pushed Fletcher's head back and directed Fletcher's hands to his pecs. Elliot was caught up in all that pleasure. To his surprise, it was the first time he'd craved for someone, or something to touch him like that, besides his current boyfriend, who had been away for months now, and was nowhere near as good as Fletcher was! He could tell that Fletcher was a maestro at all of that already, and he just discovered for himself! Fletcher started to kiss Elliot's pecs; he felt Fletcher's tongue on his already now stiffened nipples. With Fletcher rolling his tongue over them rather passionately the way he did, Elliot felt like his pecs were being worshipped by Fletcher. Elliot was astonished by the sheer ability of this blessed little guy to make him want so much more effortlessly, Fletcher appeared conspicuously a professional at it, and it was messing with his mind. Elliot was moaning out profusely. Elliot had now begun directing his head to the warm spaces between his legs. But Fletcher was going to penetrate his glory hole first.

Fletcher went on, sliding his tongue down the circumference of Elliot's already dripping erection. Elliot then felt Fletcher start to apply some pressure on his fragile but extremely sensitive uncut tip. Elliot felt Fletcher lick his tip with so much energy as though he was going to get some money in the bank as a return for his seemingly great services or something like that!

Fletcher then started to penetrate Elliot gently with his tongue, taking his time to explore the slippery walls of Elliot's warm ass cheeks with it. Elliot moaned out helplessly as he effortlessly realized that Fletcher was really good at it, and basically everything else too! Elliot had started moaning more loudly this time, as the blissful sensation felt like it got behind his skull already. Fletcher constantly mildly cautioned Elliot into trying to keep quiet more and told Elliot that he didn't need to make so much noise, even though he probably knew how good Elliot had been feeling right there. But that didn't matter much either. It felt like any neighbours he had could already hear Elliot's moans from the other side of the building space, in the other room, and if that was so, they could easily tell that something had definitely been going down there, Fletcher wasn't completely comfortable with that.

Eventually, the principal flipped Fletcher, grabbed his thick erection, slowly stroked it a little, and let his tongue find its way around his tip. Elliot teased it while listening to Fletcher's light moans from where he rested his head. Fletcher was trying not to scream out the way he had gently cautioned Elliot not to as well; he easily noticed it. Fletcher's enormous erection was pulsing intensely still as Elliot slowly sank the huge tip into his mouth and sucked on it with a bit more aggression. Elliot became hungry for it. When Elliot stopped, with the way Fletcher looked at him there, they both knew Elliot was going to ride Fletcher pretty hard, which he did without wasting any more time!

While Fletcher was lying on Elliot's soft bed there, Elliot slowly mounted Fletcher's throbbing, thick hungry erection and let it sink deeply into him all the way! And immediately, the walls of his already greased-up booty hole was filled up with this monster-sized, hard beef!

For the first time in Fletcher's entire life, he felt his erection really sink into the warm space of a male's tight hole! And having Elliot's wet tight hole grab his thick erection in all that warm, juicy goodness was absolute ecstasy! It was divine while it lasted. Fletcher moaned like a hooting train as Principal Elliot slowly went up and down on him the way he did!

While Elliot was slowly riding on his shaft there, looking at Fletcher's body build alone, with his intense imaginations still going crazy, made Elliot even more horny. At that age, Fletcher was fitter and cuter than anyone he'd ever had sex with all his life; even his boyfriend and past partners never made him feel this way! Fletcher seemed better than all of them combined, or so he thought, as he quickly went from gentle to psycho on Fletcher!

After a while of intense riding on Fletcher, Elliot started to feel the intense adrenaline rush all over his body. Fletcher was going to have Elliot orgasm really soon! And Fletcher, from the experiences he'd seen in the porn content he'd been digesting for so long, notices this and stops him dead at the moment. Teasing Elliot's nipples for a while to slow down the effect and prevent Elliot from having an orgasm that was seemingly going to weaken him to some extent.

Some part of Fletcher also wanted to taste Elliot the way he'd really wanted in his head and thrust into it with his thickness! Principal Elliot's extremely sexy nature seemed difficult for him to resist anymore. Fletcher flipped Elliot over and slowly went into him from behind, staring at his smooth skin and spotless, soft, and really bouncy butt cheeks, gently penetrating him only with his tip first, then the whole beef later on. Elliot had started to moan, still trying not to be loud, taking that thickness like it was nothing. Fletcher kept digging it like never before; it was the first time he was actually thrusting into a male without getting pain screams from the "victim" in the process; he loved it so much, he didn't want it to stop! Fletcher pounded on Elliot's butt cheeks from behind, with so much pace, energy, intensity. Getting the angles right in Elliot's wet tight hole, delivering so much pleasure, one he'd really been enjoying so much. They both lost their self-control and moaned loudly and helplessly as Fletcher felt Elliot's sweet space hold on firm into him and Elliot felt Fletcher's erection fill him up effortlessly as he kept thrusting.

A few moments later, of continued thrusting and pounding, little Fletcher's moans became more intense and louder!

He pulled Elliot's hair, squeezed his pecs, grabbed onto his bouncing butt checks, and gave one last heavy thrust before screaming his lungs out! Principal Elliot moaned profusely as Fletcher's shaft pulsed in his booty hole, filling it with his fast-flowing heated load, getting everything inside of him!

It was the first real sex Fletcher had, and it was the first time he had climaxed from a tight booty hole, ever. Fletcher wanted more; he was still hungry and tireless, they went for another round. That secret right there was the start of something rather very detrimental! While he'd gotten home thinking about it, he realized that he had just been "sexually taken advantage of" by someone who had been way older than him! His own principal, for that matter! And all of it seemed to ruin his mental health even more. His level of friends and potential sexual partners couldn't take him, and he wasn't about to start a sexual relationship with his principal! He had a little bit of a strict moral compass at the time! And that was pivotal in making the kind of person he grew up to be eventually!

Fletcher wasn't going to let anything or anyone "shame" him for his size, ever again, he decided to abstain from any sexual encounters with males, not even the older or married ones, because it appeared to him that they were the only ones who could apparently take him in the way he wanted to. He thought to himself that he had to be better than that, and he worked towards it instead.

His mother never knew of this encounter with Principal Elliot, and in all the while left to complete his high school days, he had tried his very best to resist the principal's pushes, at the same time, stay away from him and any other guy who had tried to come into his life, or into his head. And he had continued that way, even when he'd gotten into college.

When the guys would try to have a go at him and his general cuteness and intelligence, he would bluntly resist them and ask to be left alone instead!

There was Sam, Brendan, and even Troy, who tried to literally drug him just to get him laid, but he wasn't giving in easily, and he had always left them rather very frustrated and feeling powerless.

His athletic build had always been an attraction to almost every man he came across, but he showed absolutely no interest! It was just him and his dog, Ollie, against the world!

The University of Toronto had always been his dream school; he'd talked about it to his mom, and even his dad - whenever they got to talk to each other - almost every time, while he was still in high school, and even before then! And now that he was here, he wasn't about to let anyone make him lose any focus at all, or so he'd thought.

CHAPTER TWO

Sign languages and understandable gestures were all he'd communicated with. Still, everywhere he went, anywhere he'd found himself, Bobby had always turned out to be the brightest, smartest, most calculated individual in the space!

He hadn't had much of a "fun" experience all his own childhood. Unlike the spoilt and introverted Fletcher, Bobby was more willing to let his views and perspectives known! He was intolerant to senselessness, easily a Type-A grade personality, and was as handsome as anything you can imagine!

Now, it was the "official" first day of the second semester in his freshman year at the University of Toronto. He was most happy and greatly excited to resume as soon as possible and already felt that he quickly needed to get the college thing over with and move on with his life, at just his "first" second semester. On getting back to his dust-covered room space, he stood at the window side to observe the hazy morning sky as he kept on pondering on all that his overprotective mother had said to him before he'd left the house for school. It was early falls at the time, as leaves kept dropping off the trees that surrounded a small garden next to his apartment, something really beautiful that he'd always appreciated.

He then started with his usual, out-of-home routine, thinking about his family, his other siblings, his friends, and even the "haters" and bullies. Bobby was mostly a really, really smart, and nerdy person, who almost always easily blended in any sociality around him, at home, at school, and at every other place he had found himself in. As a result, most jealous and insecure counterparts constantly picked on him just for the sheer fun of it alone, even though he'd had a conspicuous hearing and speech disorder!

However, Bobby always refused to give in to any of the bullyings because he'd always remembered the promise he made to his mom that he was never going to appear as a weakling to anyone. He was always going to make his mom the proudest, even while she had been extremely protective over him.

Standing there at the center of the room, he reminisced how much of an entire journey he'd had all the while he had been waiting and dreaming of studying the arts at the university. He sarcastically went down memory lane again, thought about his first day here, when he had walked into the compound as a true freshman personality and how Lisa, also a freshman then, had happily introduced herself to him, in sign effective sign language, there at the bursary lobby. He thought to himself about how he and Lisa, awkwardly at first, then went on to become one of the faculty's most recognized couples, just after a few weeks of their full resumption.

Lisa was of pure beauty, glowing eyes, beautiful dark-brown skin, mostly petite, and just found adorable, but also had speech and hearing complications. Easily one of the hottest ladies on campus already, so it seemed. It was still of a huge surprise most times to Bobby that a lady like Lisa would get to feel anything for a regular dude like him, or it was basically because they had conspicuously shared something in common, their similar disorders! At barely 20 years old back then in the first semester, freshman year, Lisa was quite the beautiful-looking one. Her breasts had always appeared to be enticing enough to turn heads. She was almost always on her well-framed eyes glasses too. A rather very sexy slender structure always attracted the opposite gender, of all ages and sizes, students alike, and top staff, including her supervisors and Heads of Departments in college, in just her first semester. But her connection to Bobby seemed divine enough to stay clear of all that "distraction."

Bobby, though, was the first "friend" she had met in college. She noticed the sign language thing at the lobby there, from afar, while he was seeking to be attended to, and went in to make a move on him, introducing herself genuinely! Bobby instantly became somewhat nice to her and wanted the best comfort for her, which had never happened before. He always offered to help her with most of the strenuous registration tasks back then. He fell deeper when he realized that she also took really amazing photos as a "hobby", just like him! And often pushing him to sell them on various platforms, instead of just doing it all for sport! Lisa had always been an extremely "business-minded" personality, something about her that had slowly rubbed off on Bobby.

Bobby eventually found himself taking photos for the money and not just passion anymore. They would then go on to frame and auction for stores and other public places right there on campus, and sometimes, off-campus too.

He thought about how Lisa showed him all the love and care that she could. Even though she was the extremely jealous person towards him all the while and felt insecure sometimes about sit, when the ladies flocked around him each time he'd gotten an A+ in the most difficult topics, even in his "condition". He was always down for her and never wanted to let her go.

She had also been getting head-ups from almost every guy she came across with. The first thing they had always noticed was her really sexy-shaped breasts. It had always felt like these dudes were going to pounce on her hard if they had been given even the slightest opportunity, irrespective of the fact that she couldn't hear them when they had tried speaking to her. She was also pretty, with her rounded face and bright-looking eyes that always captivated male folks looking at her. She was seemingly always oozing strong sexual appeal, even without knowing it. Making a lot of them who'd picked interests in here go for their sign language courses to be able to communicate even more effectively with her. the majority of them had just wanted to get her laid, and they would go that far to get what they'd wanted, or so it seemed.

Lisa was also the first "lady" he had met in college, and her initial niceness towards him is something he never took for granted. It felt different from what other hearing and "non-hearing" folks on campus had been bringing to him; it felt genuine. Something he never took for granted. Even while they had gotten "serious", she constantly chips in the "Mister Nice Guy" sarcasm each time they got to remember how they first met. It made both of them smile helplessly.

He also thought about Wendy. The one girl on campus that hated him so much because she felt that Bobby took her girlfriend, Joanne, from her. It felt rather very funny now that they were older and more mature because Joanne, on her own, always came to communicate about how much she had felt love for him, even in his apparent condition, and how she had always seen him in her dreams, and how much she wanted to drop Wendy to be with him, by all means possible. He always tried to make him understand how much he wanted to get her breasts squeezed, her nipples sucked, and her "twat" taken care of by him. Unknowingly to him, she had been stupidly telling Wendy the same things. Prompting Wendy to always come to attack him in different ways.

Wendy became a pest to Bobby, and in turn, a pest to Lisa as well, in all the time they had been on campus during the previous semester, Wendy was the one who seemed like her entire life's work was to make Him "suffer" for his unknown "sins", and always had Lisa coming to his aggressive defense. She'd eventually gone as far as ruining his car with spray paint and making forced gestures asking him to back away from Joanne. It was that crazy!

While still sitting on his bed now, quite comfortably, he subconsciously thought about his first real sexual experience again, with Lisa, on the night of her 21st birthday. He'd easily remembered everything that happened that night. How they came into his room from a date, with her grey-coloured skin-tight gown, and him with his dress shirt and plain pants on. How he always made sure he treated her like his queen.

His first sexual encounter was with Lisa. And unlike Fletcher, Bobby wasn't hyper in any sexual activities; he'd always only considered it as "one of those things" and never took it seriously! But that night, that night was magical for them, he and Lisa. She had always come close to sleeping with some of the guys back at high school who'd been making their advances or been trying to take advantage of her then-naïve nature but always got away or lost the chance to over one thing or the other. But this time, with Bobby, everything was different or had seemed different. He always made her understand that she was always in control, that he was never going to force anything on her, and that was something she seemingly respected a lot about him!

Bobby effortlessly remembered how it all happened; It was almost complete darkness when they had come out of the bathroom that night. The only thing they could see was the lights that beamed in from outside the window, and they could feel each other's heartbeats pounding through their ribcages. The cold breeze from the window there made the "event" even more special; he could instantly recall as he turned his head to look at the same window now.

He could remember how heavily Lisa had been breathing, probably from the adrenaline rush; it felt like they could tell what was about to happen between them. Their brains were completely numb, surrendering to hormones. They were about to explore something that they had probably both been wanting to for a while. His cold eyes that night, the scent of his body had apparently made her even more unusually restless. She was about to lose control over her actions entirely. Bobby was calm, as usual, but not for a long time; some people had always said that physical attraction was not required in true love, but Bobby was always secretly of the opinion that love is like an unfinished poem without intimacy, the thoughts he had in his head. There were millions of thoughts running in their heads within a few seconds.

They had both expected it to be like some fairy tale romantic evening, but soon they realized that it would be ugly, wild, and passionate. They did not wait long to start kissing each other passionately but were mildly wild too. She made the first real move of intimacy, adult romance, with a rain of kisses on his chest, down to his groin area, and back to his chest, repeating the cycle continuously until Bobby's primal nature kicked in. He started kissing her neck in a slightly aggressive response; she went down weak on her knees. She surrendered completely to him. She felt the intense love between them. She couldn't control it anymore, she pushed him back and gestured to him gently;

"Where is the protection?"

"It" had been safely lying below the pillow. He pointed it out towards the pillow. She took out the pack of scented love gloves. And while it was in her palm, both were looking at it for a moment, with a bit of shyness conspicuously filling up the atmosphere around them. And then they looked at each other.

"Are you sure? You want to do it?" Bobby communicated back slowly while fixing his gaze on hers.

For a second, it seemed as though millions of thoughts passed right in front of her eyes. But her mind was in no position to make any decision. It was filled with hormones.

"Let's do it!", She gestured in immediate response!

Bobby's eyes broadened; there was some spark in each of them; she noticed it and gestured again, this time, a bit more aggressively;

"Make love to me before I change my mind. Otherwise, I will walk right out that door, and you won't get me in your entire life, ever again!!" teasing him with an evil-looking smile.

He remembered the fierce look on her face that night. Even he was absolutely shocked! He was seeing her "other side" for the first time, a lady's other side for the first time, something that he had no idea of, about her, or anyone at all, in their own few months of the "relationship". He was in a ride of his lifetime, or so he'd thought.

He remembered just exactly how he dropped all morals and any forms of his gentle nature and then attacked and pounced on her like a hungry lion, but she was a lioness in her own way too. He might have thought himself to be the king of her imaginative kingdom. But unknowingly to him, she would rule the bed too; it was her territory.

For the next moments, it was a pure and deadly combination of love and lust. He went on exploring every inch of her body without mercy. For her, it was basically pain and pleasure; he remembered his mind failing to name that exact feeling. With eyes closed, mild joy tears got rolling from the corner of Lisa's eyes; it was her first time too.

Rest, it was probably the direction of "love gods", to show these new love birds a glimpse of "heaven" that they had never imagined, even in their dreams. The way it was in Bobby's almost always poetic mind.

He went on caressing her whole body for a long while; it seemed that he had been enjoying the soft, joyful moans that he had been hearing her let out. He kissed her occasionally, then went back to her torso, then to her inner thighs, then back to the middle of her still tender breasts.

He'd slightly grabbed her breasts and bit lightly on her tender nipples. Lisa would always let out a light scream on every bite. They couldn't hear it, but he could tell that she was in awe of the feeling! He couldn't still properly explain to himself the exact feelings those bites always gave to her, but he knew that she loved it; he knew that it drove her completely insane! He had to remind her with gestures to not yell too much, so they don't attract any unneeded attention towards them, she agreed. Bobby was always sensitive like that!

He remembered how it seemed as though she was getting fed up with all the pleasures he'd been effortlessly dishing out on her. She, too, had apparently wanted to feel all that masculinity that Bobby's physicality had possessed. She wanted to kiss his "strong arms" like her life depended on it and lick the tip of his erection even if it was the last thing that she was going to do on the earth at that point. She did.

Watching him moan inaudibly to her actions was rather very satisfying for her in all of that silence. He moaned with every tongue action she made on the tip of his erection, leaving Bobby wondering where she had learned all of that from, with her always claiming that she'd never gotten so intimate with anyone, but now wasn't the time for questions. She then went on to stroke it on the already lubricated surface of her swollen, sensitive clitoris and entrance of her warm space, brushing it on her opening for a while before letting her little pot engulf Bobby's entire erection as she screamed in pain and hugged him tightly in a reflex response to her hymen getting pierced through. It was a painfully pleasurable experience for her. She stayed there, motionless for a while, before starting to move on him gently.

Slower at first, then she began going aggressive on him. He remembered how both of them had conspicuously moaned out loudly and helplessly in the silence of their worlds. And how he had kept trying to reach her lips with his and wasn't able to because she had completely lost control of herself; she was getting all of that for the first time! And he was, too, he realized before flipping her over to gain some control.

She had apparently moaned more intensely as his angled thrusting seemed to hit every inch of her wet walls. As he finished inside of her, spilling all of his heated sensual fluids at the end of her honey pot, he could tell that she instantly felt like she was on the edge of "heaven" and never wanted to return to earth. That was the feeling; he, too, was having, he'd always thought to himself. A feeling of outright, immense satisfaction, love in their eyes, a happy smile, and one sweet little kiss to end such a pleasurable act. It was seemingly a gift from love gods to the "honest love" they had apparently shared. Indeed, it was the best gift that any couple could receive, seemingly, Bobby always thought to himself, as he felt very graced.

His first sexual encounter was one he would never forget. And the one he loved had always been there to make sure he had a lot of it and more, till this day, he'd thought.

He was still there, at the center of his room space, looking outside the window, still reminiscing on his pleasant past experiences and smiling so helplessly to himself before a light knock on the door snapped him back to realizing he'd had been standing there for more minutes than he could have possibly imagined.

He went over to get the door open, and it was Chris, his neighbour with whom he went on to become great friends.

"I saw your car outside; why you back to school this early? There were still well over two weeks before lectures start."

"You good?" He'd said to him in the message. They communicated to each other via real-time texting!

27

"Oh no, it's nothing; I was just eager to start up this new run and get it over with, and then, get on with the next one! Plus, I'm probably excited too," he responded and smiled at him after he was done reading his text.

The two "friends" embrace each other warmly in a welcoming gesture. Chris had been his next-door neighbour since the day he moved in. He was always nice to him and protective of him as well. But surprisingly to him, Chris had never made any "romantic" gestures towards him, yet, and deep down, he subconsciously hoped that the day never came, but he had no idea! Even though he was proudly gay, Chris had always respected the people around him and never crossed the line with anyone, even his closest friends.

Chris asked him why he had resumed earlier too. He explained to Chris that he was working with someone on a piece there in school and really needed to be close to the person. He acknowledged.

He offered to help Bobby clean up his room space if he'd needed it because Chris easily noticed that it was really dusty when he initially walked in. He "nicely" declined, asking Chris to continue his stuff while taking responsibility for his own "mess". Chris obliged.

"Well, you're the man, man! Anything you say! Whatever you need, just lemme know, okay?" he happily expressed himself in the text before closing the door.

Going on to opening his bags to get out his stuff, his phone was notified for a text message. It was his mother; she was texting to check up on him. Apparently, he'd forgotten to tell his mother that he had gotten to school. She had always been over-protective towards him. Even stopped him occasionally from going on photography competitions most times, she was always cautious about his condition, and it left her worried about him all the time! He, however, had always disliked his mother for that but always had to respect her.

It was one of the major reasons he'd always said to himself that he needed to leave even the entire country and remain where he was, even after graduating college. Apart from him wanting to always explore other parts of the world occasionally, it was always also to free himself from the annoying shackles of his mother's overprotection.

"Hey sweetie, please tell me you're at least safe in your room now," she'd said to him in the message.

"I'm fine, MOM!" he replied her text with his, rolling his eyes in slight disgust afterwards.

"Okay, please do me a favour and check if you forgot anything, your inhalers? All your medications? Books? Everything?" said the response text message that came in.

"Yes, mom, it's all here, thank you," he grumpily responded after typing.

"Alright sweetie, mama loves you," said the response message from his mom, that he'd smiled at a little before tossing his phone away on his bed space!

He still grossly disliked the fact that his mother always had to remind him of his mild asthma and still treated him like a five-year-old kid all the time. Even from his early high school days, his mother would always go the extra mile in ensuring he was being monitored and "properly looked after". Something he had always found very embarrassing. Especially when some of the teachers come into the classrooms, addressing him publicly with "you know your mother said....". He had always been fed up with all that, but there was so little that he could do about it.

A few moments later, his phone vibrated rhythmically again. It was a message from his lover.

Lisa's entire existence had always felt like a blessing to him. He had always been not too sure about how it was going to come along with the both of them at the beginning, but he eventually grew always grateful for the gift. One he had never thought he'd ever get to find after his mother had always told him about how "terrible" females can be and had painted girls "black" to him almost all his life. His father had not been there to guide him on his "love choices" while he was younger and always fell for the rather sentimental ones his mother had always imposed on him.

It became even more conspicuous, what his mother had told him, in his mid-high school days, when some desperate girls would always appear to be "barbaric" on their approaches towards him, even though he was a deaf boy! Something that never ceased to amaze his mother! But them knowing he had been one of the most intelligent, yet very awkward folks among them, and also having "a lot" of people in his ever-expanding circle learning the sign language communication method because of him, and finding it rather very interesting, instead of weird. But then, there was an unfortunate minority that had always preyed on his obvious condition and bullied him for it in the process too! A lot of that comes from individuals of the opposite sex! A singular action that made him always unconsciously possess some strong forms of hatred towards girls, even from a young age. And it went on for all the while he had been at high school.

Lisa was someone who he thought had probably unlocked a part of him that he probably never knew existed. For the first time in forever, he had felt the attraction a normal young guy would feel towards a girl; was it because of their similar disabilities? Or his rather very attractive cerebral capabilities? Or the fact that she had been the first person to show him such care, attention, and probably genuine love? Or the sexual tension that always drew them together? He would have never known.

She was his first true love. One he had never seen coming. And so far, he was still happy and proud that he allowed himself to love her back. He had no regrets yet.

While smiling helplessly as he looked at the phone vibrate after a while, he eventually picked it up to respond to her texts.

"Hey bubbles, what took you so long?" The most recent message said.

"Oh, oh, it's nothing, love, I was just here absent-minded for a while, I'm sorry about that", he responded in soft empathy.

"Okay, well, good morning!" she texted again.

"Yeah, guess who's back to school?" Bobby asked excitedly in his reply.

"Well, isn't it obvious?" her text said.

"right, so how about you? When you gonna be showing up, love?" he asked in his message to her.

She went on in a rather long composition to explain to him that she wasn't going to be showing up at campus anytime soon and that she had been really occupied on some business that might cut into some of her school time too in the process.

She'd talked about the new "business" she had ventured into and told him that she would be well late to campus resumption this time, even after the lectures would begin. She went on to tell him bluntly that she needed to get back to work, ending the conversation with him.

Bobby was devastated on learning that he wasn't going to be spending the few weeks before the lectures had begun with her. It was the other reason why he had left home so early. He was instantly let down emotionally.

He was worried about how the next few days without his lover would turn out to be like. He laid down on his bed in extreme emotional fatigue, staring at his grey-coloured ceiling, wondering how he was going to quickly recover and accept the sad reality that was standing in front of him before hearing another knock on the door. He went over to open up; it was Chris, again.

"Ohh, what now?" Was the gesture he unconsciously let out to Chris before seeing his text notification.

"Hey man, I'm so sorry for the disturbance, and I see you're probably stressed too. Haha. Maybe I'm the last person you actually want to talk to now, but...."

In a rather very long composition, Chris was inviting him to a disco party downtown, not too far away from the campus space, for him to get a chance to unwind and ease up some stress over a few drinks.

"I'm not sure about how I feel right now, so I don't really know about that", he almost bluntly responded in his text message there, while standing in front of Chris, still wondering why Chris couldn't just text from his room instead of having to come over and make him open the door and stand there in front of it.

"Oh, trust me, man, it'll be fun, and I'll show you the sticks too, that's in case you're really a newbie," Chris said to him sarcastically in the message.

"Alright, alright, fine. I'd come. If I don't feel better after that, I'm smashing your windscreen, man!" Bobby responded in his text message.

They agreed on an 8 pm time, and he shut the door afterwards.

He figured that he was going to do more of trying to catch up on academics in the time he had left before the lectures were to resume so as to brush up on any slacks he had probably been scared of coming across as the new semester went on.

He'd thought about Professor Fred. His new mentor in arts and photography, one that Bobby had come really close to because his daughter was also non-hearing. Hence, he had to learn the sign language efficiently too, making communication between him and Bobby always smooth. He had given Bobby a holiday-long project to work on the previous semester. A photography documentary about bees. He thought about how he had been busy with all of that throughout the holiday period and knowing how strict Professor Fred had always been when it came to his works, Bobby was always most careful and did not take it lightly.

Although Professor Fred had always stated it to Bobby, sometimes sarcastically, sometimes very seriously that he had really liked him, with a strong sexual attraction that even he couldn't explain, and would have loved Bobby to give him a chance to make him "happier" than he had currently been, helping with his grades and also, "extra activities" too. As a young, rather very cute and hot man too at the time, discretely between them, the professor was always "shooting his shots" from time to time but always focused on what had needed to be done.

He continued to unpack his stuff from his bags and placed them where they were to be in his spaces and closets. He thought of himself as being prepared for the new but vast journey ahead and was ready for any challenges that came along. Despite his physical condition, he always loved challenges, and that character had kept him fighting all the while.

It was almost 8 pm; it seemed sooner than he had expected. He realized the time and quickly hopped out of his bed and into the shower. He picked up a nice pair of blue crazy jean pants and a plain white t-shirt to match. He still didn't quite know the real nature of the party because Chris hadn't given him much of a "description". So he decided that he was going to look as basic as it gets for this one. He thought of telling Lisa about the "party", and what he was going to probably be doing there too, but then realized that it would be better if he wasn't texting her to give every detail now that she was on to some "serious business".

Just as he was putting on his strong polished vine-scented perfume, his phone vibrated; he picked it up, suspecting that it was Chris, looking forward to getting him ready, he wasn't wrong. In the text, he stated that he was at his door waiting and that he was with someone, not delving into any details, only to get to the door and meet Ashley, Chris's boyfriend. They hugged each other happily before Ashley went on to explain that Chris had told him that he was available and decided to come to say hello to him too. Bobby was moved and thanked him in exciting gestures.

It was time for them to leave for the venue; Bobby went on to take his pair of glasses before Chris quickly objected and let him understand that he would not let Bobby go with glasses this time. Giving Bobby his pair of dark-shaded sunglasses instead.

"If you're scared of the light, this should help yo ass," he said to him via text before letting out a burst of visible laughter and bumping Bobby slightly on his shoulder.

They then step out together, down the stairs, past the hallway, out the building, then into Chris's car, a Dodge Charger SRT series. Ashley requested that he drive because he had always loved the feeling he got from driving such muscle. It "made him hard", so he always claimed.

They drove off to the party center, where it had been conspicuously going wild and crazy. More than Bobby had possibly imagined. The music was pounding loud, but Bobby couldn't hear a thing. The other people had dressed in different costumes; the dance hall was a huge space. Bobby fell shy immediately; he hadn't been the type to attend such "mega parties". And with him subconsciously knowing that the people he actually came in with had been in "a pair". He wasn't sure about how it was going to turn out for him; all of that was happening right in front of him, for the very first time.

They got a spot to relax, and Chris took the drinks responsibilities. He was the extreme corona type of person, and the same was his boyfriend, Ashley. On the other hand, Bobby wasn't always keen on consuming alcoholic content at all. So he had requested plain fruit juice instead. Something that Chris found extremely boring.

"Oh, come on, man, it's the party! You gotta unwind, let yourself off, have a great time!" the message from Chris read on Bobby's phone!

"Don't worry, man, I'm not interested", Bobby texted back in blunt response.

"Oh no, I AM NOT GETTING YOU PLAIN JUICES", he responded in the text to Bobby after shaking his head and walking away from them to go bring the drinks over.

"You know you don't always have to be like that, right?" Ashley typed in the message he showed Bobby on his phone, then watched him nod to it.

"It's a party, not a conference meeting in school, you know. Unwind!" he added again

Bobby tried to communicate to Ashley sarcastically in blunt sign language, making some fun of him in the process, knowing that Ashley didn't understand anything he'd been trying to say to him, and then laughed out loud!

"Very funny, right? You got jokes, bro! Now look, you got to get a hold of your life and do the things that you actually want to do, man, Lisa, or your mom, and the others don't control you, one bit! You're smart enough to make decisions for yourself now, man, and you know it, not leaving with rules of someone you don't even know what he does when you not there with him". Ashley put to him in a rather slightly lengthy draft.

Bobby then grumpily agrees to all Ashley had said with a continuous nod of his head to prove. In a few moments afterwards, Chris walked back to the table with a few cream liquor bottles and tossed the one with the mildest alcoholic content to Bobby while he and Ashley go on to drink up theirs rather carefree.

Bobby took the first sip. It had been his first time consuming any alcoholic content without the "supervision" of Lisa, his most trusted "entity". Chris easily noticed his sluggishness towards the drink from across the table where he and Ashley had been seated.

"Hey... Drink up, unwind, free yourself. That bottle was an expensive one for a special dude like you. So, don't sleep on it!" he said in his text to Bobby after noticing he seemed reluctant with his own "dose".

Fed up, for the most part, Bobby decided it was high time everyone stopped peeking on him and saying things like that to him over some "petty drink"! He quickly gulped up the entire bottle content and requested Chris get him some more.

"Oh yeah! It's ON!" yelled Chris, inaudibly to Bobby, before quickly stepping down to go grab some extra bottles.

Chris seemingly let his "guard" lose and got drinking rather carelessly, unknowingly giving in to the pressure of the other two. And when it was time for everyone to get dancing, the DJ turned up the tempo! Chris and Ashley then went on to the hall center to grab a dance together, in awe of each other too, unknowingly leaving an extremely tipsy and slightly horny Bobby behind. Alone and not able to hear all that had been going on around him there, he'd had no other option than to sit back and watch them do their thing! He thought to himself, there was no way he was about to approach anyone and tell them that he was deaf and could only communicate via texts or sign languages. Lisa would have been a great pair partner for him if she had been there, but unfortunately, she was absolutely NOWHERE near him at the time, and that ensured the littlest chances for him to get laid at all, with the way he had been feeling!

A few moments after all their fun and probable exhaustion, Chris noticed that they had apparently made a mistake bringing Bobby along with no plans at all to keep him engaged while they had been having their own fun time, he asked Ashley to join him in moving Bobby out of there, in case he was stoned from the drink he'd been having. It was time for them to leave! And as Chris had predicted, Bobby seemed really unable to properly carry himself when they tried to walk him out of there. Ashley had to almost completely support his footsteps all the way back to the car, and Bobby had been completely stoned! On getting to where he had parked the Dodge, Bobby unintentionally threw up on him. Being a completely clean freak, Ashley freaked out immediately and tossed him to the ground in complete disgust.

He yelled at a stoned Bobby for doing something so nasty but realized that it wasn't necessary later on. Chris then warned him to go easy on Bobby and persuaded him to understand that it was obviously Bobby's first time experiencing stuff like that, consuming so much hard drink. He let Ashley know that he was still worried about Bobby doing anything rather stupid later at night and even suggested him staying with Bobby for the night, too, if possible!

Chris managed to clean him up, take him into the car, and then carefully drive them back to the apartment building. Luckily for Chris, Bobby was now able to walk when they had gotten there. He managed to get to his place, opened the door, and collapsed to the floor at his entrance. Chris, who had already been at his door, heard the fall and came rushing to his aid.

He had regained a little more of his cognition but wasn't "strong" enough to move. When Chris turned on the lights, Bobby's entire state became more visible for him to see. The vomit had also stained his outfit. He looked at Bobby and realized that there was no way he was going to shower up all by himself in this condition. He carried Bobby into his bathroom space and gestured for him to get himself cleaned up.

Bobby then gave him signs that he needed some privacy, and that was when Chris was convinced that Bobby could do the bathing, at least, on his own. So he left the bathroom space, through the room, then out through the entrance.

CHAPTER THREE

It was a bit hazy outside his window as he'd slowly opened his eyes to dim daylight the next morning, while his puppy had crashed all of its tongue and saliva on his face, whining helplessly because Bobby had completely forgotten to give it lunch and dinner the previous day. With rather very strong headaches that he had been feeling even in his dreams. He knew he had a terrible hangover and couldn't even remember just how exactly he got to the bed or much of anything that happened after he saw Chris and Ashley having their moments together, back at the party space. But he could tell that he really needed to feed the poor pup.

He slowly got up and went over to his bag to look for the aspirin pills he had come home with. And then went serving some good dog food. For a while, he got really disappointed in himself, thinking about the fact that he let himself fall for pressure of anyone at all. At first, he decided he was going to tell Lisa about it since they basically always told each other whatever "odd things" had happened to them. It had been the first time he was getting tipsy without her, the first time his libido had gotten to those heights without her, but then, he didn't know just how he'd managed to scale through all that! But then, he debunked the idea instantly. If Lisa doesn't know, it won't kill. He thought to himself.

It was a Saturday morning now; he knew he was going to have to clean up all the dusty closets and furniture and get on moving his stuff from his bags to where they were supposed to be. While doing that, he felt his phone vibrate. It was Professor Fred. He'd had a really frustrating hangover; he didn't want to communicate to anyone at the time. But he knew he had to reply to the professor, at least.

The professor had been reaching out to check up on him and ask how the "bee project" had been going. He surprisingly answered all of his questions effortlessly, surprised that his texting speed hadn't been affected by his ugly hangover. He reminded Bobby that everything he had done was supposed to be ready before their lectures had resumed fully as it was going to be the first thing he would check. Bobby concurred and rounded up with his professor, nonchalantly dropping the phone back to the bed.

He finished his cleaning-up activities and thought he needed to get some fresh, cool air. So he decided he was going out to try the skiing resort upside of the campus space, one he'd always tried to go to the previous semester but was always too busy and lazy at the same time, but now, all that steam needed some blowing off.

He laid down on his bed to relax his back for a while. In less than a few moments later, he hopped off the bed then went over to some of his still packed-up outfit bags to quickly reach out for a heavy sport-centric outfit. He took out his thick joggers, a skin-tight grey coloured hog to match, and then a heavy sweater, coupled with sneakers.

He made his way through his door, then the long hallway, through the building entrance, then out on the cold streets as he started counting steps from thereon. He noticed that the place had become a really peaceful neighbourhood without so many students to always wreak some havoc as he made his way in-between streets, with his little pup beside him, to his destination.

On his way to the top of the reserved ski resort, he noticed his pup swerving in another direction towards another dog that it had seen coming close to them, pulling its owner as well—awkwardly forcing both dudes to gradually run beside each other while their dogs had been getting some social time for themselves down there below them.

"Staying fit doesn't seem too difficult for a tough guy like you, huh?" he asked Bobby mockingly, as he noticed he was struggling to maintain the pace they'd been with initially. Bobby didn't see his mouth movements because he'd tried to keep his eyes fixed in the direction they had been running in, leaving this temporary partner slightly dumbfounded.

At this time, he was vividly getting exhausted already. And the pace seemed to slow down as he was obviously now pulling on his dog to slow down.

"Oh, seems like you don't do this pretty often," he said to Bobby, inaudibly.

"Hello!" he yelled with a wave of both his hands to Bobby, the single action that got his attention!

Bobby had to apologize in his best form for him to understand, and that was when the other guy had realized that Bobby was deaf.

Stunned but impressed and heartfelt at the same time, he made a gesture to Bobby, asking him to remain calm and stop jogging in the heavy snow if necessary. Requesting for him to have to sit there for a while, with a soft smile. So Bobby did, while their dogs had still been having their "moment" beside them there.

He gave Bobby his phone, and when he looked at it, the text read, "I'm Fletcher, nice to meet you!"

After nodding his head, he typed in his own name and gave the phone back to Fletcher.

"Bobby, that's a great name, man!" Fletcher exclaimed inaudibly to him before pulling him up for them to have a go at it again.

After a few moments taken for Bobby to beat the snow off his body, he seemed more motivated to go against this Fletcher guy again! His initial niceness had gotten to Bobby, and he couldn't explain why Fletcher had left a slight dib on him. There was something about his charisma, his sheer will; it bloomed well enough for Bobby to notice!

While they had been going about it, Bobby felt himself shutting down slowly after trying to endure with keeping Fletcher's pace for so long! And after a few seconds, later on, he collapsed softly to the floor, prompting Fletcher to stop dead in his own tracks and go after Bobby, on the snowy ground behind him, struggling to catch his breath, laying basically "helpless".

"You just might be needing another set of lungs, huh? He said to him sarcastically before unconsciously reminding himself that Bobby was deaf!

Oh, my bad," he said to himself softly as he reached out to him and pulled him off the ground again, awkwardly trying really to make any meanings in the sign gestures he was making to Bobby. Bobby shook his head in sarcastic disappointment as he handed Fletcher his phone so he could type in anything he had wanted to say right there on his device; he did. And responded with a simple "Yes, I guess."

Their dogs had still been into each other, conspicuously enough for them to realize. Fletcher had been more outspoken now than he'd been in the early stages of his life! He pushed for conversations more now, sarcastically talked about anything he felt like or noticed.

He saw Bobby as a man with a "good heart" and considered him "cute" too. He'd requested that Bobby exchanged contacts with him so they could talk more and sarcastically added that he had already grown tired of typing in messages on Bobby's own phone, a statement that effortlessly pulled a smile out of Bobby's already frustrated-looking gaze! He agreed. They go on to exchange numbers, and texting between them was seamless, immediately!

Bobby easily noticed that Fletcher had more "athletic" than him and had no business trying to keep up or even compete with Fletcher in any way whatsoever. So he decided to "back out" of the chase and let Fletcher feel as good as he probably wanted deep down, or so he'd thought.

He watched Fletcher come even closer to him and realized even how physically fit Fletcher had been, noticing even more conspicuously the slight bulge in-between his legs. Bobby tried to take a step backward, then tripped and fell back to the snowy floor. Landing on his butt cheeks had him realizing how really weak his legs had been after such "strenuous" activity. He beat himself up for trying to match paces with this new guy, but the deed had been done already, and he'd had enough of the "oppression". He'd thought to himself sarcastically. An amused Fletcher came in to pull him up again.

"Damn, He's huge," he thought to himself when he noticed the large bulges of pure muscle on Fletcher's body, especially the one in between his legs, as he watched Fletcher come to lift him from the ground for the third time in a few minutes, and then, sat up to properly engage him in a "satisfied" conversation as they went on.

Fletcher was the more engaging one among the both of them. He then told Bobby that at that point, he was an aspiring basketball player for the county's basketball team. Still introducing himself "properly", he continued by saying that he loved to joke around with "kids", too. He already seemed like a video game person to Bobby before he had even started mentioning all the titles he had then bragged about. Not suspecting any reasons why Fletcher seemed really open and upfront towards him, he seemed to enjoy the short conversation with this "stranger" already. Seemed like a great guy.

They got really "talking" in a short while, exchanging rather very engaging and intelligent conversation topics via their texts, there, sitting close to each other the way they had been, and both their dogs still doing their own "thing". Bobby didn't know exactly why, but he had been unconsciously finding this Fletcher dude really hot and physically appealing. His muscles seemed like they were well-chiselled, down to the very last detail.

He started to feel some "strange attraction" at once! He wanted to be like Fletcher; Bobby loved the way Fletcher's physicality had appeared like, which was something that had never happened before, even he was surprised too. They'd instantly got along right there. Fletcher was more on the rather very friendly side toward him too. It turned out that he lived in an apartment a few blocks away from Bobby's. They had light conversations as they subconsciously both agreed to forget about the "ski adventure" they had originally come for. Then, they slowly walked together and made their way back to the street where Bobby had stayed.

It was an eye-opener for Bobby; he had painfully realized how terrible his physical fitness had become and how really "amazing" some strangers might turn out to be so "nice" to him and not feel any forms of immediate intimidation all of that. He was happy where he was.

When they had gotten to Bobby's block, and it was time for them to part ways "temporarily", they realized that their dogs had become really bonded that they noticed the conspicuous sadness on each of them! The dogs whined uncontrollably in dissatisfaction, as though they had really known that it was time for them to say goodbyes to each other. The dogs and the new friends did as Bobby slowly made his way into his apartment block and watched this new "Amazing" person walk away to his own destination.

Bobby sat down on his soft bed on getting back to his own apartment to ponder about what had happened back there. Why was he "restless" on seeing the size of Fletcher's "monster cock"? How did he get to flow so well with just some guy that decided to join him jogging? Why had he been smiling helplessly to even Fletcher's bad jokes? He was confused. He hadn't felt so much pull to someone other than Lisa, his first "true love" and apparent "girlfriend". He thought that it was probably her unavailability and missing her "companionship" too much that had made him feel that way. But even at that, Fletcher was a dude, and he wondered why he had been sensing a "start of something beautiful" with Fletcher. He was as perplexed it sounded, but then, there was only so much he had real answers to.

In a few moments, after he'd had his breakfast, his phone rang out. He suspected that it was definitely going to be the Fletcher guy. He picked up his phone to check; he wasn't wrong.

They had then gotten texting each other for a long while over the phone. A few minutes eventually turned to an hour, and they didn't seem like they had wanted to stop either. Yet, right there in his room, he had been feeling less lonely already, effortlessly accomplished by someone he had only just met on his way to apparently just blow off some steam that day.

On the other hand, Fletcher had been enjoying this new guy's company all along, surprisingly! As a rather very reserved personality, he wasn't the type to make new friends easily, but this, this was different. He couldn't explain why he just wanted to keep tabs on his new friend. The "new friend", although couldn't speak, had already seemed like a great personality. He had only been there at the ski for the second time since he'd resumed there at the university. And it seemed like he had just made a "real friend" for the first time.

Although he had been sleeping around with some "more mature" college ladies, and those are the ones that could take him!

He'd even had a romp to attend to that night as well, with an older woman named Sarah, one of his really attractive lecturers on campus! They had been talking about their sexual encounter more times than he had imagined, and had even secured a "location" for the whole thing, an open space, slightly away from his block, where no one would get to notice any of that, what they were going to "perform". They'd had some "moments", at any little chances they had. But then, it would be cut short as a result of "unforeseen circumstances"!

He'd whiled away some time communicating immensely with Bobby that he didn't know when it was evening already! And the rather very punctual Fletcher beat himself up for almost completely their time window, he and Sarah! And he had quickly gotten prepared; his outfit, perfumes, energy drinks, and his "perfect sex playlist" had been placed where they ought to be.

He made it there in time, early enough beat her to getting there first! And waited for her "patiently".

And when he noticed Lecturer Sarah showing up to where he'd parked his car, he flashed his headlights a little, letting her know that he was the one in the rust bucker and that the "location" was secure enough for them to do their thing!

But then realized that something was odd while she had been approaching closer to him. She wasn't in the best emotional state, and it had been written all over her face!

He got out of the car and asked her what the problem was. She explained to him about the really bad day she was had been having! First, a misunderstanding with her best friend, and then an office disappointment had ruined the entire day for her, and she wasn't happy at all, but she knew she had to come to see him altogether, she needed him to make her a bit happy, take all that frustration away for the day, hopefully!

Fletcher was sensitive enough! He understood his "assignment" and knew that he had to "get to work" immediately! He held her softly, enveloping her with a warm kiss, trying to calm her down a bit! Right there, just like the other times that they'd been repeatedly interrupted, the spark between them seemed "reborn" and "unchained". Although Fletcher had been in it all just for the fun of it, Miss Sarah had already started developing rather very strong emotions toward him! The warmth from their lips, colliding against one another, and the taste of the burning attraction sparked up into heightened libido really quickly! She kissed him back!

He graced her with more kisses on her forehead after pulling her back to face him. She raised her head and lips up for another deep kiss from him, he concurred. He slowly carried her to where he'd parked his car, a few feet away from where they had been standing

In the haze of the evening, with no one around them, alone, leaning on the side of his red-coloured Chevrolet car, they kept kissing each other passionately and got more intense eventually. With the way the lip lock had gone, they knew they wanted more! Memories of the past kicked in, and the primal craving enveloped them!

She felt his erection grow rapidly in-between his thighs; she groped it with her palm immediately. He then carried her and placed her on the hood of the car and blessed the top of her chest with the warmth of lips, and then started to feel all of her breasts and nibbled her nipples with his bare hands, slowly massaging them as he went on! It had been just like before, but this time, there was going to be no one and nothing stopping them! Fletcher couldn't keep himself from filling his mouth with as much of her breasts as possible. Miss Sarah got moaning again as she held tightly to his head while he was still handling her breasts. He flipped her over to lay her breasts against the cold surface of the car hood and then reached out to the space in-between her legs, locating her already dripping and waiting for its opening! His erection throbbed even more in his pants; primal urges raged as he got slapping her labia area with his tongue from behind her; he explored her clitoris gently in ways that got Miss Sarah trembling helplessly.

He then paused for a moment, and when she would helplessly and desperately imagine that he was going to stick his 11 inches into her next, he would tongue her again. The cycle continued for a few moments until she helplessly screamed, "Please Fuck Me, baby!" again. Fletcher had eaten her from behind so good; she could no longer control her cravings; she wanted him, now that they were completely alone after a long week, she wanted it, all of it, all of him, and she was going to get it!

After more tongue strides and helpless moans, Fletcher eventually slid his stiffness into her warm, wet pot, with a mind-blown Sarah helplessly grabbing her own hair while moaning out even more loudly!

He went on thrusting into her, slowly and steadily; Sarah's moans easily filled the entire open space, echoing and with her gasping out with every thrust of his shaft into her as they went on. He grabbed onto her breast from behind her to feel them, succulent enough as he kept on thrusting, filling up every inch of her slippery inner walls.

Fletcher's thrusting into her became more fast-paced, on his car hood there, as he began to moan out loudly in absolute pleasure. Sarah had felt his legs shaking behind her. He was going to climax soon. He realized his lecturer's warm space had been so tight that it hugged his erection well enough to blow his mind! He felt the tight and slippery squeeze on it with every thrust. He had loved every push of himself into her. It was a feeling he had never wanted to come to an end; the nostalgia was beautiful all the way too! Miss Sarah had "tasted" so good!

After moments of now fast-paced thrusting into her, he quickly stuck out his stiffness and sprayed his heated sensual fluids all over her back area and bouncy butt cheeks. It seemed to Sarah that this orgasm had hit him really, really good because she could hear how loudly he had been screaming, and it went on for longer, longer than anyone she'd ever heard.

His "size" was impressive enough; it drove her crazy as well, but she had been taking men his size too before him, and it had been nothing new, or so it seemed. This was Fletcher's first sexual encounter in a very, very long time; it was obvious to her that he had been trying to catch his breath afterwards. Oh my, that was really good! He whispered to the side of her left ear while he'd still been trying to recover from the intensity of the orgasm!

A speechless Sarah didn't respond to anything he's said to her at that point, she wanted her orgasm too, and there was no way she was going on with whatever they were going to be doing without her achieving it! Although Fletcher also made her realize just how much she'd really missed a good "size", but she still wanted more and more she was going to have!

With Fletcher still directly on top of her, on her back, trying to figure out how she was going to get cleaned up, he got up gently, reached out for a clean shirt that had been at the backseat of his car, and wiped her soiled body parts with it, softly apologizing for the mess he had seemingly created afterwards!

When he was done, she held him, paused to catch his gaze for a moment, and smiled at him lightly; he smiled back, in awe of the glare in her rather very beautiful eyes. He could really tell from the look in her eyes that she'd still wanted some more of what she had just gotten! He could tell that she's probably missed it, all of it, and it was conspicuous in the way she looked at him and in her body language! He leaned in to kiss her again. Slowly and more passionately this time. She started to moan under her breath again. She held him tightly to herself for a while before trying to reach out for his pants to pull them down completely, not showing any concern of where they were or worrying about if anyone was going to walk in on them there or anything like that, the way it ought to be!

They sat up, off the hood aggressively to rip each other's clothes off. Fletcher, watching his lecturer's breasts bounce off from her bra cups, rushed in to give them a hard squeeze while using his tongue on her stiffened nipples again; he never had enough of them! She moved her entire body in rhythm to his pace. She moaned out as he kept on tonguing her hard nipples still. She felt her wet walls get even warmer and more slippery and filled with more fluid beneath her; right there, she realized again how much she had actually needed it, this feeling, pleasure, without even knowing. She unconsciously pushed his head towards her labia area again. He knew what he had to do.

Fletcher went down on her again, licking each side of her inner thighs for a while before going on to bless her tender clitoris with his wet tongue and lips. He would brush his lips against the hood of her clitoris and flip his tongue around it in a circular motion, taking his time now, more slowly, and continued the cycle to listen to her helplessly move her body and moan out in extreme ecstasy. He then moved up to her belly button area to caress her torso for a moment, only to have Sarah pushing his head back to her pussy.

After a few moments of "eating" her rather properly, he flipped her over to catch her blissful gaze and flipped her to her side, on his hood there, with the moans and yells of pleasure still echoing in the lonely space, it appeared that no one had passed that space all the while they were doing their thing, and they didn't seem to care about that, their hormones were in control now, and they had submitted to it helplessly!

Fletcher gave her bouncy butt cheeks a few rounds of loud, light slaps and pushed his erection into her warm space gently, from behind her again. Sarah gasped out loudly in pleasure, as always. She had missed all that goodness after such a long day; she hadn't been penetrated this good by anyone in years. The last person she could think of was her ex-boyfriend, who'd promised to get married to her, then, she'd realized that he'd strongly belonged to some drug cartel and had to let him go! From someone she had already been having strong emotional bond with, this feeling was divine! Or, so it had seemed like.

Fletcher was good at his own sexual game, and it was conspicuous enough! Sarah shut her eyes tightly in pleasure as he kept thrusting himself into her from behind her, and when she would want to flip herself over, he held her back in place.

"You are not doing anything; I'm pleasing you alone today", he whispered gently into her ear.

He maintained a slow pace as he kept going into her from behind, there on the hood of his car. He watched her butt cheeks wobble with every thrust he made, to his utmost visual delight.

He increased his pace gradually, only to listen to his helplessly pleasured lecturer moan out uncontrollably. She was in heaven; she was on top of the world, under him; she was being pleased beyond her own explanation.

Each heavy thrust brought Sarah closer to orgasm! The way Fletcher grabbed her hair, massaged her spine with his tongue and breath, and her breasts with his other hand made Sara feel like the earth beneath her was slowly moving away! Exploding in aggressive pleasures, she felt her pelvic muscles contract uncontrollably as she let out squirts and more screams after her climax had rained on her, while she expelled fluid from her honey pot with Fletcher still digging and holding her to the hood firmly!

After more aggressive thrusts into her, Fletcher climaxed too, Again, spilling his heated fluid on her smooth butt cheeks while he moaned out loudly in utter ecstasy. The mutual feeling was divine. Motionless, she laid there, still trying to get over the pleasures that had just been served to her. She was very satisfied!

It had been just a few moments of laying on the hood together naked before they'd heard multiple footsteps approaching from the short, almost completely non-visible distance; the pair quickly hurried off the hood, then into the car, and shut the doors in a bid to hide their unclad selves from whoever had been walking by! Precautions taken, as they both watch each other burst into laughter over what had just happened

After almost two weeks of fantasies and uncontrollable urges getting the best of them, for such a "long time", they had finally battled it out, they had finally "felt" each other, and in Miss Sarah's intentions, all of that goodness wasn't about to stop between them anytime soon! She wanted something from him, more than him being just another mere sexual partner! His "size" remained one of the most impressive she'd ever seen, and she wanted to keep it!

Bobby and Fletcher had still been keeping healthy and intensive communication between each other! In the few days after their "first meeting", they had gotten to know each other, and now, the two new friends wanted to see each other again. Bobby had wondered why he didn't get to notice Fletcher all along; he was just a few blocks away.

As the weeks slowly went by, the boys each realized that they had become rather very great friends, partners, and maybe, "brothers."

Fletcher's jokes made Bobby laugh in ways that left Bobby always shocked and feeling weird about the whole thing! He was always "craving" to hear from Fletcher to make him laugh feel more comfortable with himself and all. Lisa hadn't reached to him since the last time they texted each other. And he seemed to have gotten carried away by Fletcher's niceness and couldn't help it.

It was Friday now, and they had both agreed on going jogging together again the next day. Bobby did not know himself as someone who'd get down looking forward to seeing a friend again the way it was with Fletcher! He couldn't explain why or how it had been happening like that, but it was! It was the first time he had ever felt that particular way. Despite the "connection" he had to his own non-forthcoming girlfriend, he had found something "Special" with Fletcher, and it wasn't scary; it felt good. Bobby had probably and unconsciously wanted something different. But all of these feelings were still under study; he wanted to be sure of every step he was taking along the way, always wanting to be in control, or so he'd thought!

He had been reading some research pieces on his computer when he felt his phone vibrate. It was a text from Chris; he was at the door. He had come to spend some time with Bobby after being absent, not even coming to check up on him all week, the way he usually would. Unknowing to him, he had been kept company all the way by the "new guy". And he was happy too. The first thing Chris noticed was Bobby's slightly nonchalant attitude towards him. Bobby appeared to be unusually more focused on what he was doing than on Chris. It was odd to him because Bobby was always very happy to see him. Chris understood that he should have expected any of that because of what had happened a few days back, but not in the way that he had seen Bobby go on.

"You good, man?" He subtly asked in his text message after relaxing in.

"Never better, man, just studying," Bobby replied.

"How about Ashley? Hope he's good too?" he continued.

"Ashley's great too! He'd had some intense school drills all week, and I've been a lonely asshole all the while, too," Chris responded in attempted sarcasm.

"Alright, man, I'd check with you later, kinda occupied right now", Bobby replied in a seemingly blunt manner.

A slightly numb Chris then acknowledged with a soft "okay" before moving out of the space and shutting the door.

Bobby didn't seem to notice even Chris's facial expression and kept on with what he had been doing. He had found a really interesting topic that he wanted to really explore in a different culture and overseas, film-making.

The next day came by, and he woke up the rather very stormy Saturday morning. He instantly knew that there was no way he was going jogging that morning. He then checked in on Fletcher, and he was about to see and experience the same thing. So they both decided to cancel the plan and opted for their routine texting conversations over the phone instead. Only this time, they went from basic conversations to rather personal and subtly "erotic" ones in due time, where all of it had seemingly headed to. Bobby told Fletcher about Lisa, and he told Bobby about his own "stories".

Fletcher spilled the "beans", teasingly explaining to Bobby that this was the first time he's shared such a bond with a person, more especially, a fellow guy like him, and confessed that he had absolutely no explanation about all that had been happening! He went on, assuring Bobby that he had never felt so much "attraction" to anyone until he found Bobby. A statement that struck a nerve on Bobby because he wanted to take it all for an adult joke, but even he could tell that all Fletcher had said wasn't out of the picture, he too, had been battling with questions about what was really going on between them all week. Questions about how all of it was ever even possible! He and Fletcher hardly ever had physical contact apart from the moment when they had just met each other back at the ski resort. And now, they had been secretly really looking forward to seeing and meeting with each other again!

It became now certain that he, too, had been feeling even if it was slightly the same way about Fletcher; it wasn't one-sided, it was mutual. Unexplainable, but unquestionable. The "tension" between them started to build up from then on.

Lisa had still not contacted Bobby since then, and when he would try to reach out to her through the texts, she'd seemed non-responsive. Bobby got worried about her and decided to reach out to her friend Alexa to ask about her whereabouts. It was then that he was made to know that Lisa had actually been at a party that night, even at the moment that he had been texting. And that she was "unavailable" at the moment. On the surprising side, he'd then went on to ask Alexa about Lisa and her "business", only for Alexa to go on asking him what business he had been talking about.

Unknowingly to her, Lisa lied to him about whatever she was really down doing and didn't get to ask Alexa to cover up her tracks for her on that end. Lisa had probably didn't expect Bobby to reach out to Alexa for anything, but then, he did.

Alexa went on talking about how Lisa had been partying around, hanging out with some illicit dealers and personalities over the past weeks, and having a great time with her new sexual clients. Bobby angrily tossed his phone to the floor. Bummer.

He was devastated at the fact that Lisa, his "everything", had lied to him and kept asking himself for possible reasons. Wasn't he good enough? What had he done to deserve such a form of betrayal? He asked himself sadly as strong confusion set in even before the real anger and rage came.

He yelled inaudibly to himself as he went to his bed, hitting his pillows on the frame in utmost disbelief before calming himself down. In the short time they had been together, he had always trusted Lisa with everything he had. And getting to know that she had lied effortlessly to him like that was a deal-breaker for him. He had never expected her to go on do something like that to him, ever! The betrayal.

He decided he wasn't going to try reaching out to her anymore. Letting himself free from having to care about her so much while she had been there doing her thing. Plus, there was Fletcher now, who quickly seemed like he had valued Bobby and had a "thing" already for him too. And considering that the feeling was seemingly mutual, Bobby subconsciously decided to become completely carefree about whatever Lisa had been doing, wherever she was. He had been pushed to tackle Alexa's claims about what Lisa had really been doing, but he had no choice as Alexa had sounded innocently convincing, and Lisa hadn't even picked up his calls or replied to his texts to clarify or confirm anything whatsoever. He bluntly decided that he would refuse to feel any form of remorse for anyone who had lied to him or made him feel that way. Including Lisa!

In the few days of him meeting up with Fletcher, Bobby started getting to see new perspectives on life then. Gradually, he was no longer just the nerdy, deaf dude down the hall or the awkward dancer in glasses. Fletcher always talked about how Bobby's charisma always rubbed off on him and regularly asked Bobby to "keep up with the good work" as he was bolder now, thanks to Bob. In such a short while, Fletcher had seemingly taught him things that Lisa, the plain" lover girl", probably couldn't. Fletcher had even let bobby in on his Royalty secrets, but then, dismissing any assumptions of him ever taking up any monarch responsibilities at all, subtly asking Bobby never to try talking in him into any of that, sarcastically assuring Bobby that he was going to fail miserably at it!

CHAPTER FOUR

College activities had fully resumed, and lectures had started promptly full time. More students were now being seen at the apartment building, and life was back to a proper normal in no time. It had been weeks since the last time Bobby and Lisa had an actual conversation. And ever since he had found out what she had really been doing all the while, he had since appeared non-interested in her. Fletcher, on the other hand, seemed to have been advantaged by his "unfortunate" emotional situation, and it was rather easier for him to "get into" Bobby's head and then into his "confused" heart. Fletcher always went for what he wanted, and Bobby wasn't out of the picture, unsurprisingly to him. His only issue" though, was how Bobby was going to cope with his "size" then things would start to get really heated up between them

Wendy had returned at the time too, Bobby had once more accidentally bumped into her at the faculty building, and just when she expected Bobby to hurriedly apologize calmly to her, the way he would have always done, she got a blunt "hey, watch where you going" sign gesture from him as he walked past rather nonchalantly. Wendy was a bit surprised by this act as it immediately felt like Bobby wasn't "cautious" of her anymore. She decided that she was going to confront him some other time.

Most of his friends had now noticed that even his "walking pattern" had changed and that he was now even more social and daring and less "all-academic" than he used to be; some liked it, felt less academically intimidated by the deaf dude, but some others had been more interested in finding out what the "problem" had really been, all of the new characters was off what they'd know Bobby would usually stand for. This caught the attention of even Chris. He went on to sit Bobby down for a conversation and softly asked him in the texted conversations about what had "really" been going on. Then Bobby broke it to him that Lisa had given him lots of reasons to now "be free" and live his life to the fullest. He went on telling Chris about how Lisa had helped him maintain some "strong levels" of morality all the while throughout their first time on campus and all of that. But now, she's conspicuously abandoned him. Making Chris understand that she hadn't been communicating with him all the while, despite him always trying to reach out almost all the time. He told Chris that he wasn't going to disturb himself anymore. Until she probably sees it fit to come to fix her mess or at least contact him.

Chris was confused and could tell that whatever the case was, Booby had made up his mind to go down doing whatever he really wanted to at that point. He pleaded for Bobby to be careful in anything he was doing and told him that Ashley had really wanted to see him too. He seemingly concurred and left Chris there.

He went over to an apartment block to see someone who was "very dear" to him as well, Tricia. She had obviously resumed lectures alongside every other person, and Bobby felt quite bad for not keeping proper communication with her until this moment. Sadly, he needed to vent a little bit now and hoped she wasn't mad at him. On getting there to Tricia's apartment, he knocked lightly on the door, and Tricia immediately freaked out on seeing him as she'd opened up the door. A rather very jovial soul, she was.

"Oh My God, Bobby!?" She exclaimed inaudibly!

"Oh my God! Tri, you got fat!?" Bobby gestured in a rather very surprising stance!

"Come one in, come on in," she gestured back happily!

Tricia knew some sign language and even tried really hard to perfect it in such a little while! Although there was an instant bond between them, too, not romantic at first, Tricia couldn't keep her cool with him, but then had to "respect" his relationship with Lisa at the time and didn't go any further in making romantic strides toward Bobby.

He happily obliged to her welcoming gestures and went in. Unlike Bobby, Tricia was almost the direct opposite of him. Academically care-free, now lesbian too, alcoholic, and whatever you could think of. But she had always had a soft spot for Bobby still, and even she didn't know why. Although her sexual fantasies leaned towards Wendy and her lover and always had even come up bluntly about it to them, she had always wanted to have a taste of Bobby still. Tricia constantly found herself learning from Bobby and always wanting to "be like him. Bobby had been of great influence to Tricia without him even knowing about it.

She served him a burger after hugging him for possibly the tenth time before they got on "discussing". Tricia was the talkative one of the two friends. She had always had something to "say" at any time. She would always talk about the new girl's "pussy she ate", or the guy with the "biggest dicks she'd fucked", or how she had always wanted to have a feel of Bobby's warmth deep down, trying to sound sarcastic, but being really hopeful about it deep down. Tricia was on the very beautiful side too. Her dark skin with black hair always stood out everywhere she went. Her butt size was on the bigger side; she was also "thicker" than Lisa had ever been, and she had always secretly hoped that flashing it to him the way she did was going to get to him the way she wanted it to!

Bobby had requested a "hard drink" in a short while afterwards, something really strong to get his mind away from some "stuff". She concurred, not minding to ask him about the reasons for his drunk urge, but she wanted some of that goodness at the time too; she got the bottle of hard rum from her fridge and served it alongside her own cup too. Tricia wasn't sure if he could handle the alcoholic strength of the drink he's been having, so, all the while, had made sure that he was going to engage in anything "stupid" as she started to feel some level of instability in her head and slight loss cognition too due to the heftiness of the drink, she didn't know when she had taken too much! All had been going calmly and under her control until Bobby drunkenly groped her butt and hugged her from behind, when she had tried really hard to walk over to where the fridge was to return the bottle. That single hug had her get a direct feel of his dangling erection throb in-between her soft butt cheeks!

Bobby had been "stoned", and his libido had been "thinking" for him at that point! While being really tipsy too! At the time, she could tell that he had been really "wanting" and needed that comfort and relaxation from her too, and even while she was willing to give it to him there, the fear of the non-pleasurable repercussions still drowned her thinking; she was a nympho, an aggressive one at that, and wasn't sure of his sexual prowess, and how well he could handle her, even now that she was as drunk as what she could imagine! She thought about all of that before gently pushing him away; she wasn't ready to be left "horny" and helpless and craving for more after he's had his orgasm. A rather very tipsy Bobby then gently came back to grab her breasts, this time aggressively. Tricia was a bit stoned now, too and after the breast grab, felt the tingle in her body, in between her legs, the rush of warm fluid, quickly filling her honey pot up, and impatiently waiting to be penetrated by him, or anyone, or anything at all!

She quickly made her way back to the bed while gently dragging him close behind her; the craving had become unstoppable! Finally, they got into the moment; this was going to be the first time they were going to be having a sexual encounter and Bobby's first actual drunk sex! She felt like it would be relieving for the both of them in the long run, from their own respective frustrations.

Without much further ado, she quickly stripped him off his clothes and gave his erection some good, warm tongue thrusting till it became completely hard as a rock, the way she had wanted it. Then, she gently pushed him to the bed with her index finger; she was going to ride on him aggressively, not minding if he was going to have an orgasm quickly or not anymore! She was now at the height of her libido and needed to get something inside of her, and that's all that mattered then.

She was riding on Bobby as hard as her body could take her; although "average" as it was, she still felt his erection slide through the walls of her warm essence and started moaning subtly. She didn't expect that he was going to have the notion of flipping her over because she felt he was completely wasted at the time! She was flipped over very easily; he stroked her dripping opening with his thickness for a while, then went inside of her again, slowly at first, then aggressively as he went on!

His moans got louder than ever; she tried tightening and "locking in" her vaginal muscles so she could feel more of him while he had been going in hard on her warm tube! Her moans weren't as loud as she had wanted them to be! She felt like she wasn't getting the full experience; she was helpless enough! And after one last full thrust, he involuntarily ejaculated into her, filling her up with his warmth while screaming uncontrollably and then collapsing aggressively to the bedside afterwards.

Unsatisfied and still drunk as she was afterwards, Tricia headed to the bathroom to try to please herself with her vibrator, and as usual, it was as "useless" to her as he was at the point. A sexually frustrated Tricia then had her shower and came back to meet him already sleeping, and then she had no other choice than to join him. Mission accomplished, although not one hundred percent.

Tricia was always one of the ones standing up for Bobby when he had allowed himself to get "bullied" by Wendy, her secret crush, on many occasions, and now, she'd finally had sex with him, underwhelming as it was, the sheer thought of it alone had been rather very satisfying.

He'd spent the rest of the day there before heading back to his own apartment. When he had gotten his "normal self" back and could still remember all that happened between him and her, he had quickly rushed in to apologize to her and promised her that they were going to have a go at it again some other time and that he was going to make up for the "terrible" experience she'd just had with him. She concurred.

He was still happy to have gotten to see Tricia again; he needed that relief, sure of the physical and emotional one, but didn't know about the sexual one. But he knew he had to get back home to prepare for the presentation he had the next day with Professor Fred. He had earned his respect all the while for being one of his most distinct and smartest students, and he wasn't willing to let the Professor down anytime soon. Chris came to check up on him again that evening, in the hopes of having a conversation with him about how he had seemingly changed over the recent days and wanted to be sure if everything was alright with him. On getting to his room, with the door being left open by bobby, he realized that Bobby was as very occupied as he looked and couldn't have the "conversation". Bobby also showed him afterwards that he had important stuff to take care of the next day, which meant that he needed time to himself to do what he needed to do. Chris let him be.

When he was done finalizing his presentation information, he texted Fletcher. In the conversation, Bobby talked about how important this piece was to him and how grateful he was going to be if he scored an actual A. A rather very happy Fletcher tried his best to motivate Bobby over the phone with his rather respectful abilities of wordplay. Something Bobby had subconsciously held special too. Every word that Fletcher had said to him, he did not take for granted.

In a few moments, after he was done talking with Fletcher, he phoned his mother and told her about his progress and how he'd been all the while. It was then that she broke the news to Bobby that his younger brother had been in a severe car crash. Explaining to him that it was why she hadn't reached out to him all the while, she apologized for keeping such information from him for such a long time. She explained in the texted conversation that Barry, her brother, was now doing fine and recuperating well, though. Bobby went from tense and angry to relaxed immediately. And thanked his mom for "being there" for all of them and promised her that he was going to make her proud and make up for his father's current absence.

The next day arrived, and an excited Bobby rushed over to prepare and head off for his presentation. He had no atoms of doubt or fear as he always considered himself extremely smart, confident academically, and well above his equals.

He got to the office of the professor. It was the first time he was seeing Bobby after lectures had started for the semester. He easily noticed how "bigger" Bobby had become since the last time they'd seen each other.

"Wow! What has mama been feeding you with?" he gestured to Bobby sarcastically.

"Oh, regular food, and lots of love, Sir", he replied to the professor while giggling uncontrollably

He asked Bobby to come on into the office, closer to him. He went over and sat down closer to him, on the opposite side of the table. Bobby goes on to receive more subtly, rather "erotic" compliments from him, which he innocently smiled to, unusually, before going on with the presentation.

It was a huge success. Professor Fred was mostly mind blown at his capability to perfectly understand and explain entire concepts and perspectives of the topic he'd been given. He outdid himself very well. And got the professor completely impressed, as usual. He easily decided that Bobby was going to be his favourite student that year. He'd secretly had other intentions too. To have a feel of Bobby and his sexuality, if he ever had the chance to. He was absolutely turned on by such brains, handsomeness, and sexual energy.

He got back to his apartment afterwards and told his friends about the leap of progress he'd made. He'd told Chris, Tricia, and his other fellow students. They were most happy for him, as always. He contacted Lisa to at least let her know and share in the excitement; Lisa wasn't accessible still. He found himself getting worried subtly but then remembered all that Alexa had told him; then, he shook off the feeling. He told Fletch about it too, and he decided to "celebrate" with Bobby that evening.

They agreed that Bobby would come over to his place later that day and maybe even have a sleepover. And when the moment came, they found themselves not being able to "resist" each other, giving in to the locked-up emotion and denied attraction between them all along, in all that excitement, and it didn't feel weird, not one bit!

Bobby had remembered the size of Fletcher's thickness he had seen on him that other day and couldn't keep his cool each time he pictured it; he had some strong urges to touch it, stroke it, feel it, kiss it, and maybe, go even crazier with it. Fletcher, on the other hand, had the emotions too and was very open to trying something new with Bobby; even though Sarah had been there with her urges too, he had tried his best so he could get to eventually explore his sexual possibilities with Bobby and see if he was worth keeping since the feeling and attraction had been conspicuously mutual. They "wanted" each other that night, even more than they had both imagined, and they could conspicuously see it.

Fletcher was rather very good with his cooking skills; he served Bobby a very "nice dinner" with some white wine to "celebrate" him. And Bobby didn't hesitate to let himself get showered with all that "care" from this special attraction interest of his. Apparently, he needed it too. Fletcher's apartment was more on the simple side; the walls were in a monochrome grey-looking hue; the interiors were colourless and mostly grey too. It seemed to Bobby that Fletcher had loved monochrome colours a lot too, and it affected his basic taste of everything. Even his plates, mugs, and wares were either white or grey or silver.

They'd had dinner together and gotten relaxed in for the night before Fletcher went on asking after Lisa. He quickly noticed that Bobby wasn't interested in talking about Lisa either. Leverage for him to "take advantage" of that night sharing the moment.

The texted conversations grew long and less interesting as time went on. Bobby noticed that and unconsciously fell into feeling really sleepy, as already very exhausted as he was. He asked Fletcher if it was okay for him to lean on that huge chest of his for a while. Fletcher effortlessly concurred and watched Bobby going on to lean on him on the couch there and stared at the ceiling for a while, trying to adapt to the new "paradigm", his submission to a guy that he liked so much, and feeling completely comfortable with it, a rare blessing, it seemed.

CHAPTER FIVE

'C'an I kiss you?" Fletcher asked carefully in a texted message.

Bobby picked up his phone to check and saw the message. Then, slightly surprised at the question, he sat up and caught Fletcher's "burning gaze" and let out a mild smile before agreeing to it and then nodded his head.

"Why not?" he responded in his message.

Bobby knew the tension between them had grown immensely in such a little time; he just didn't know how much. And since Lisa had been a dick all the while, and Tricia still not in the complete picture, he'd felt abandoned and emotionally unstable until Fate seemingly brought in Fletch to pick up the pieces, or so it seemed. So he was happy Fletcher asked the question, and he couldn't explain why he was anticipating it.

After a moment of looking into each other's eyes, Fletcher leaned in and moved his neck forward, softly brushing Bobby's lower lip with his before pausing to look at him again. Bobby kissed him back! It felt good! Real! True! Like nothing he'd ever felt before! He quickly realized that Fletcher was a GOOD kisser, way better than Lisa or Tricia could ever be! He instantly felt Fletcher's tongue constantly scraping the roof of his mouth and going deeper before he stopped, maybe to take a breather or something as he asked in soft gestures;

"What are we doing?"

Fletcher couldn't understand what that part of sign language meant, but he could tell that Bobby seemed unsure about the action they had just taken. He felt the intensity of the kiss and could easily predict where all that energy was eventually going to head to! And didn't look like it was coming to an end any time soon either!

He pulled Fletcher back to kiss him again, quietly and slowly still, expecting it to be even better than it was previously; this time, things got a little bit more intense, they got aggressive, Fletcher pulled off his now-moistened lips from Bobby's. He went straight to Bobby's neck like he was wired to do it! Bobby loved the feeling! He watched himself start to moan lightly, inaudibly, as Fletcher's tongue slowly found its way across the areas of his neck that drove him crazy, so crazy that he had started to moan a little bit louder! His "sound" was one Fletcher had grown to admire already.

It was as amazing to Bobby as it seemed, the whole thing, the feeling of sensual fulfilment, turning him powerless. He wished to stop and get a hold of himself but couldn't; Fletcher understood that Bobby just might have been getting a hard time giving into this seemingly "new" paradigm, and acknowledged that he needed to take things between them, the obviously burning attraction, rather slowly instead. Fletcher took Bobby's head away from his shoulder and asked him to get his shower and relax his head on the pillow afterwards.

After the shower session, in Fletcher's conspicuously cozy bathroom space, Bobby was given one of Fletcher's shirts to wear and a thick cardigan for the seemingly cold night ahead of them, and, just in case Bobby wasn't comfortable with sleeping "naked" on the bed with him. Bobby rejected bluntly and insisted that he was going "skin to skin" on Fletcher that night.

"Goodnight", Bobby gestured understandably to Fletcher as the boys kissed each other again deeply for a moment.

They went to bed under the grey-coloured duvet, dim lights that had atmosphere in the room cozy enough, and slow music that had been on a low volume, playing in the background. Easily Fletcher's type of thing!

He opened his eyes to rather bright daylight, and soft RnB music had still been "playing at a low volume in the background" there. Bobby instantly noticed that there was a "nice scent" in the air he'd been breathing. Fletcher had been in the kitchen space, preparing some breakfast for them. Bobby walked over to the bathroom space to take a morning hot shower, it had been cold degrees that morning, and some "heat" was needed, apparently

And when he'd come out from the shower after a rather very hot bath and met some fried potatoes with hot ketchup and coffee waiting for him on the center table in Fletcher's living room, he was absolutely pleased on realizing it seemed that Fletcher was "most concerned" about his "comfort and satisfaction", both physically and mentally as well. Bobby then went on to the table right from the bathroom to enjoy the meal that had been seemingly waiting for him while it was still hot, not minding if it had been actually his alone or not, conscious selfish behaviour.

"How you feeling, 'princess'?" the text from Fletcher asked softly on his phone while Fletcher had watched him eat

"This is good, really good. Where'd you learn to cook?" Bobby has paused to ask happily with a mouth full of fried potatoes as he'd also realized that it wasn't just some "regular" or averagely made potatoes and ketchup. It looked and tasted different. He felt like Fletcher had some "special recipe" to it that was different from the usual or regular fries he'd always had.

"Oh, that? I always worked at an eatery in downtown Wichita during summer holidays back at high school days, and other things as well, haha", he said with an assuring smile in the response text message sent to Bobby.

"You like it?" he continuously asked Bobby in the follow-up messages, innocently.

He watched Bobby nod his head aggressively, and a gesture from him that seemed like a loud "yes".

A few moments afterwards, Bobby realized that it was almost 11 am, and he needed to prepare for the lecture session he had that day at his faculty. He quickly told Fletcher about the lecture session and convinced him that he'd really needed to leave immediately.

"We'd continue this later, Fletch." He said to him in the message sent, with a smile on his face before picking up his clothes from where Fletcher had put them.

Fletcher sat in wonder of everything that had just happened between them the night before as he watched Bobby change into the clothes he'd come there with at the corner of the room. He was in awe of how such a seemingly nerdy and calm dude, or so Bobby had portrayed himself to be initially, managed to get to his interests. Fletcher couldn't shake the feeling of strong attraction he had been getting right there, and it was mutual.

Even though his original plans, unknowingly to Bobby, was to use him as another mere "sex toy", just for his own fantasy sakes for a while, as this was his regular lifestyle, he decided within himself that he was going to keep the emotions he felt towards Bobby for a long while instead. An emotional experiment.

On the other hand, Bobby was more on the light-hearted side, purely emotional, and with completely clean intentions. And when he was done with changing his outfit, the boys game each other a warm hug, and then Fletcher watched Bobby gently step out of the door and then headed to where he was going.

On getting back to his apartment, he felt his phone vibrate. It was his mom. She was always reaching out to check up on him as the only kid she'd had away from home at that point. Although Bobby was always fed up with her overprotective nature most times, he was always grateful to have a mother such as her. This time, she had reached out to him to tell him about Barry's recuperation. He was most happy to know that his brother could walk again after mom had told him that the doctors had said that Barry might not have been able to walk properly again. He felt most happy for his little brother. He immediately reminisced on how close they had really been as kids, how he was always the smartest and nerdiest human entity in the entire home, even with his hearing problem. He remembered what it was like to always have to be the one to take care of his brother's little "sorry ass" when everyone had left home for their respective duties. He remembered how uneasy it was for both of them, especially Barry, when they lost their father in a car crash. Barry had been their father's favourite kid. Bobby remembered how jealous he was of Barry to come to take his former spot as their father's favourite kid. Now he escaped possible death or complete paralysis, and Bobby found himself crying subtly in an emotional outburst.

Over the phone conversations there, mom could tell that he wasn't completely okay and knew that she had to make him feel better by promising that she would not let anything happen to Barry and assured him that they were going to be okay.

As usual, it was a long, hectic day with the lecture session. Drained, as he walked into his apartment space, he was almost immediately followed by Chris, who wanted to have a conversation about how distant he had felt like they had gotten. But, again, he realizes that Bobby had been in absolutely no mood for that, so in his texted message, he just jokingly asked

Bobby about how his day had been before asking about Lisa and got shocked at how he responded.

As he laid there exhausted on his bed, he had bluntly told Chris that he wasn't interested in. However, his "precious Lisa" had been doing anymore! Since she'd decided to go on living her life without even telling him about her decision. And then, him having to go on living his life too, Bobby explained bluntly in his replied message. Chris went numb immediately. Wondering about how possible it actually was for Bobby to go on making statements like that to him.

He wondered what had happened and why Bobby just changed into being so "brutalist" and cold in what felt like all that change had happened just overnight. The same Bobby that had been so down to earth with the love of his life and always bragged about it as though it had been them against the world was now sounding this way about the same lady? Chris was "speechless". He tried to pick Bobby's brains by asking him who he had been moving around with now that made him so nonchalant and less concerned about Lisa, the one that he once couldn't "do without"?

He bluntly communicated to Chris that it was none of his business right now. And he should let him relax for a moment, trying to state how tired he really was. Chris obliged. He thought to himself that it was probably because of the recent alcohol intakes that had probably been messing with Bobby's brain, or maybe because he now felt rather "grown-up" already in the second semester of his freshman year in college. Either way, he hadn't seen Bobby like that before; he wasn't sure how to react to it.

Bobby had not much to do the next day and went over to Chris's place to apologize to him for the slightly rude attitude towards him the previous day; Bobby was still empathic. He explained to Chris that he had been really exhausted for the day and had no strength or will to see or talk to anyone at that point in time. Ashley had been present too. In no time, they'd all embraced each other and apparently "got along" again, making up for the lost time and probably the seeming slight hole in the relationship they shared.

Bobby then went over to see Tricia, his craziest friend. He told her about Fletcher and what had just happened between them, and how the new "experience" was. Talked about his sexual "size", the way the kisses hit differently, and confessed that he'd enjoyed it really well, better than what Lisa had been giving him all the while. He let Tricia know that he was confused about having to start "something serious" with Fletcher or not, claiming that he had never been so pleased before. Tricia welcomed him to the "same-sex" club first, sarcastically, then went on advising that he shouldn't go rushing in all because of a couple of good kisses. She narrated an experience of hers to Bobby, about a girl she had met two years before, about how she was loving and extremely "caring", how she'd sexed her good and took great care of her, and how she even made promises of them getting married eventually. Only to find out that the girl had done and told the same thing to five other girls. Tricia made Bobby understand how devastating it was to her. She claimed that's she couldn't eat for days and that it was hard for her to ever really fall in love again, even till that moment.

Bobby was of the strong opinion that whatever it was, Fletcher was different; it just seemed true, how they'd connected, he had felt it! Just a kiss from him, but it felt like their souls collided right there in the act, and he saw it in Fletcher's eyes too. He stood convinced enough. Tricia warned that he should be careful before changing the topic and moving on to her smoking spree, which Bobby couldn't seem to stand at that point. After a few moments, the friends then exchanged pleasantries, and Bobby left, feeling rather very relieved that she didn't bring up the topic of their previous encounter.

CHAPTER SIX

Their time together throughout school was a huge one for the boys, the girls, and everyone else. Bobby and Fletcher. They had thrived academically, Bobby more. He had matured in ways even he had never thought possible in such a short while. Fletcher's influence had now rubbed on him completely. He found himself thinking and acting differently. His self-confidence had heightened exponentially. Fletcher had taught him to dominate too, instead of always being "dominated", boosting his already heightened self-esteem to its highest points. A paradigm that even Wendy quickly noticed and now realized she couldn't mess around with Bobby anymore, for any reason at all. He had changed his glasses frame into a more "trendy" one, replacing it with the awkward-looking one he'd always worn before. His sexual appeal grew immensely. Out of all the ladies who'd been coming his way, Tricia had been the only one getting the stick when she wanted it throughout his time at college. Although not completely satisfactory, it was better than not having his sexuality at all! What other girls had conspicuously wished for!

Even though they hadn't gone down dating each other yet, he and Fletcher, the way he might have probably predicted, the kissing and caressing was the heaven for Bobby! Over the years, they'd gotten even closer to each other as they went on, had their "special moments", had erotic kissing sessions in the bar, on the beach, in the garden at night, name it. Bobby apparently couldn't control his lust for Fletcher. He wanted to actually "date" Fletcher in a mutually official manner, but Fletcher always constantly relented, and Bobby couldn't explain why. And even when he felt like he was going to be able to "do away" with him for a while and get his stuff with Tricia going, he had always found himself uncontrollably running back to the tip of Fletcher's lips. Helpless attraction.

Fletcher and Miss Sarah had been secretly still doing their thing with no strings attached (rules by Fletcher). Even she wanted something serious happening between them eventually, but it only ended in emotionless orgasms and boosted marks at school for his "perfect" services to her! No one had "touched" the way Fletcher did! HE had grown to be a man who knew how to touch a woman! And he did it perfectly, effortlessly. Miss Sarah had proposed the idea of them getting married to him, but he always shot it all down! Bobby was a man in his own heart, and he couldn't wait for what the future held for them. Miss Sarah hadn't been in the picture.

Chris and Ashley became the only friends Bobby could really confide in, all the while at college. The rest of them had moved on to enjoy their final year seasons in the other different ways they'd deemed best. Wendy now showed more regard to him and almost had sex with him, with a "foursome" between them, he and Tricia still in contention., Bobby had now become a completely "no-nonsense" person. And it became easier for her to see the day Bobby descended on her in gestured aggressive outburst, outsmarting and outclassing her right there at the center of a campus garden for everyone to see, with a translator stepping in to interpret every "attack" Bobby dished at her hilariously, to the apparent entertainment of everyone who had been watching.

Just like that, he had seemingly lost complete contact with Lisa. A small part of him was still always worried about what had happened to him, he was always in contact with Alexa, and she constantly told him that even she didn't know what Lisa had been up to lately. He slowly realized sadly; it was time to completely move on with his life.

He had constantly improved his photography skills now; he had been mentored by Professor Fred, whom he had always told about his filmmaking dreams. He found himself in the professor's special care and encouragement space all the while, from start to finish. He told Bobby that he was going to give him the chance to direct some theatre plays and that he was going to make that very possible with his influence.

Bobby had always wanted to be a director. He'd always had ideas and concepts in his head that he'd always wanted to bring to life. He would always bring new dynamics and angles for the professor to see, and he was always impressed with the capability of such a "special guy" with no prior directorial training. And by the end of the semester, he was now getting screenplay from the Professor's contacts to work with. Bobby decided he wasn't going on break for the semester. He was going to start work on those projects immediately.

Fletcher had been there for some psychological and sensual support all the while; the lip locks were always mind-lowing; it eased both of them off any stress they had been going through all, as they'd always told each other. And by now, Fletcher noticed him getting more occupied with assignments than ever before. Bobby wasn't as disposed as he used to be; the time always spent between them had dwindled drastically; Fletcher was not bothered because he understood that Bobby had to work; he understood that this was Bobby's passion, one he had always talked to Fletcher about. He always gave Bobby space to do his thing.

Fletcher's future was already "secured". His monarch father had made plans for him already, and Fletcher didn't really have to do anything much or work hard for anything at all. Even his final session projects had been all breeze. The "easy life" was all around him, and with Miss Sarah getting all she wanted for him, he'd gone through the entire school system like a knife through butter.

Bob's mom kept reaching out to check up on her son, giving him all the emotional support he could get. Barry was now fully recovered and was able to go back to being completely okay! It had seemed like everything was finally back to normal.

Bobby decided that the chances he now got in directing from the Professor were a huge new step in the right direction. He found it as the probable start of his wanted career in directing. He saw himself as being more focused on his works than anything else. He won't see Chris, or Ashley, or Tricia, or even Fletcher for weeks; he won't have any sex or kiss anyone at all for weeks. It was from his apartment to his theatre, working on himself, trying to be the best in his own way, even though he was deaf.

When the projects eventually kicked off full time, he realized handling people and professionals, in real life, in his condition, wasn't as easy as he had thought it would be. Bobby met with new people, different personalities, philosophies, cultural heritages and initially found a hard time shaking all of that at once.

Eventually, he found his bearing and was able to absorb all the pressure. Professor Fred had introduced him as "gifted and extremely talented". In no time, Bobby was handling these projects effectively, with his now-trusted translator, Stan, as not everyone could understand the sign language gestures he had been giving, and not everyone was ready to take directions to a scene or act via texted instructions. He was directing and overseeing campus-wide huge projects already. He met with different professionals from different schools, particularly Owen, a friend of Fletcher's too, and a young professional photographer and aspiring filmmaker. He was from New York in the USA. He had fallen in love with his works in a short while after Fletcher had kept sending pieces of them to him, asking if he was interested.

Owen had first heard about the buzz of a deaf boy always churning out top-notch content for his campus' theatre plays but didn't take it any seriously initially until he had recently seen the actual video of one of Bobby's directed stage plays from Fletcher. For reasons unknown to even him, He decided to travel over to Toronto to visit the school and get a chance to see Bobby in person. He Did.

On getting to finally meet Bobby at his faculty for a brief conversation, and maybe, personal interview, he quickly admired the energy in Bobby's voice; the look in his eyes had felt like Owen had seen diamonds, even his moans while gesturing was melody to Owen's ears, his well-styled hair waved with the breeze, as it flowed down a bit to the left side of his face. The "haze" in his eyes caught Owen's attraction the most. To him, Bobby was bold, "beautiful", sexy, and apparently very talented at the same time. Owen called Bobby the most handsome soul he'd met!

After a brief introduction and exchanging contacts for easier texted conversations, Owen pleadingly requested a coffee sit down with him. Bobby obliged, stating that he had been in a hurry and was from Fletcher but had time for that.

"Sorry to bother you or take your time but, I heard about you and your works from all over the place, and then Fletcher mentioned you!" Owen's texted message had read.

"I got to see something rather amazing in the 'Beautiful Orchard' stage play you made. I loved it!" Owen continued excitedly.

"Oh, that's one of my three so far; I look forward to doing more too", Bobby responded very promptly.

Owen then went on to introduce himself as an aspiring filmmaker too and told Bobby that he would really love for them both to work together now or in the future. Sarcastically assuring Bobby that if it took him learning the sign language for them to understand each other better, he would!

He had told bobby that his dad was a professional director and producer of international movies and big-budget content too and promised to use his influence to leverage for their mutual support.

Bobby immediately grew interested. He saw a huge opportunity in everything Owen had said.

"Plus, I like you too; we should get to know each other better," Owen added teasingly.

"Oh, thanks. But we're going to work, Sir, and not play", Bobby replied sarcastically.

He made Owen understand that he had to finish his college degree program before embarking on any other thing. Owen promised that he could wait. Stating that there was something about Bobby that fascinated him—claiming that he really wanted to be a partner with Bobby and his creativity. And also probably wanted to get to penetrate him as well. He couldn't seem to shake Bobby's "beauty" off his mind. He had been on a plain t-shirt that day, so his attractive slender structure, coupled with such handsomeness and caliber, Owen was aroused by Bobby, effortlessly!

Owen, also with his rather slightly slender physique and not so appealing physicality to Bobby in any way, was from a rather wealthy background, so he had wanted to come down as capable of making those "dreams' of Bobby's come true. And probably in the process, get to have a taste of his sexuality as well, not knowing that he and Fletcher actually had a thing going on already

The boys then exchanged even more "pleasantries" as Owen gave Bobby his card and Bobby gave him other phone numbers for contact variety.

"Have a nice day, Sir", Bobby gestured softly before moving to get off the chair.

A dumbfounded Owen didn't know or understand what that had actually meant.

"That was sign language for 'have a nice day, Sir'", the text that came into Owen's phone from Bobby's read!

"Oh, where are my manners? Call me Owen, Owen Braxton." He texted back sharply.

"I really have a hang on this sign language! It seems I am gonna have to pick up some pace then!" He added in a follow-up text!

The boys then shook hands before Bobby walked out of the coffee place. Owen stood there for a moment, watching Bobby move gently and smartly as he walked down to the exit. Bobby was oozing sex appeal, he thought. But he was more in admiration of the plays he'd heard that Bobby directed. And he was going to hang around for a while to watch him and observe how he had worked on his sets and learn a thing or two about his "methods" for free.

The next day, Bobby was to go on a now–routine directional duty. His phone vibrated; it was a message from Owen.

"Good morning. Can I see you today?" he'd asked, appearing as gentle as possible.

"No, I'd be down busy, Sir", Bobby replied bluntly.

"I know! I also want to watch you work, learn a few things from you, and observe your methods before heading back to New York. I wanna tell my dad about you." Bobby responded.

"Oh yeah? Okay then, I'd send you some directions," Bobby responded sharply before dropping his phone for a while to stretch a little bit.

He went on to text Owen the location of where he was going to be doing his directing that day. To his surprise, on getting to the place, Owen had already been there. Watching him let out a slight wave and left Bobby a bit confused.

Owen's phone buzzed as he watched bobby approach him, still in his smart-looking walking steps!

"How did you...?" Bobby's text had said before he had eventually walked up to Owen where he had stood.

"I have my ways, but never mind," Owen Responded.

"Now get to work, knuckle head." He teased.

Bobby let out a smile before walking away.

Owen was quick to notice the passion and determination Bobby had worked with. Bobby's level of control and subordination was one he had never seen from a deaf, still young folk such as Bobby. The way he moved and demonstrated, and then his translator saying all he'd been gesturing while demonstrating the scenes, were all perfect, in complete sync! The way he addressed his crew, down to the way he gestured "action"! One that everyone had seemingly understood easily already, at that point. Owen was turned on instantly. All that he had seen created huge amounts of respect in him for Bobby. He wondered why Fletcher had kept Bobby away from him for so long, when there was so much potential in what he saw, and questioned him for it! In Fletcher's defense, he'd told Owen that Bobby had only started the whole "director craze" even recently, stating that even he had to give Bobby some "space and time" to focus on his projects, knowing that it was his passion, and he was all out in full support for Bobby, Fletcher. Owen was determined that he was going to tell his father about Bobby. He was absolutely satisfied with what he had seen.

After the work for the day, he cornered Bobby to rain down praises on him over what he had seen him achieve. He confessed he had never seen such young talent in a while and from such a "special" person at that! And was instantly down with the idea of potentially having to work with Bobby eventually.

The texted conversations were awkward to Owen because he'd never had to "forcefully text" the person who was right next to him for basic communication purposes! Owen requested access to Bobby's plays that were on video so he could take them to his father to see and assess. Bobby easily obliged. Owen told Bobby that he was heading back to New York soonest and would reach out to him when he could, also in regards to Bobby's work. Bobby was most pleased. Owen moved in to give Bobby a hug, he welcomed. To Bobby, it was just a mere gesture of appreciation. To Owen, a rare opportunity to feel Bobby hold him, the closeness, what he was really after.

Professor Fred had now regularly been telling Bobby how proud he was of him. He stated that he initially put all that as a lesson for Bobby to learn and improve on, never knowing that he would turn out so good. By the start of his final semester, Bobby had been getting Emails from different theatres to assist them in their various contents. He had grown so popular in a few weeks. He had been so good; it took him days to wrap up directorial duties and coordinate perfect rehearsals. His new crew and Stan loved to work with him too. He was always easily one of the smartest people in the room, if not the smartest person. So he easily earned a huge level of respect.

Lisa, his first actual "true love", had been in his past now. He'd never thought it, him and her, was going to end up that way, but it did, young as stupid as they both had been. The way she'd seemingly ghosted him and claimed to be busy with "business" now felt like some seriously funny bullshit to him. He had now met and mingled with more people that constantly took his mind away from any of that. And he was good at it. He was now getting even erotic compliments from people he had never thought he was ever going to have to relate with. His extreme self-confidence slowly invited mild levels of unhealthy ego in the process too.

All that while, he hadn't had any sex or sensual moments or even thought of it. And whenever he and Fletcher had texted over the phone, he seemingly didn't respond to Fletcher's usual dirty jokes and general sarcasm the way he was seemingly supposed to. But Fletcher understood. He gave Bobby all the space and time he needed to do his thing. Chris had seen how he would always leave the apartment early and come back in really late at night. He was more worried about Bobby's physical and mental health. Bobby had always told him that he would be okay each time Chris showed acts of care.

His mother kept strong communication with him all the way too. While being aware that her little deaf boy was now being stressed out like that and making a few bucks for himself, a little bit more professionally gave her some levels of peace of mind too.

It was the weekend, and He decided he would spend it at Fletcher's place, some time, long enough for them to "catch up" with each other. Fletcher was most happy to see Bobby again, after so much time spent away from each other. Not as if they had actually been dating or anything like that, but they knew they had a soft spot for each other already, and it was real and true; they both could feel it!

On seeing Bobby after opening his door, he watched Bobby smile in a huge, slightly awkward excitement before kissing him. He kissed Bobby back, right there at his doorstep. The kiss was a deep one, they weren't going to let go of each other's lips immediately, and they knew it. While still kissing each other deeply, Fletcher stretched his hand to shut the door behind Bobby, lifted him from his legs, pulled him up by the butt, and carried him slowly to his bedroom space. The sexual tension and intensity between them rapidly heightened right there! Fletcher already appeared like the "dominator" between them! He seemingly couldn't wait to force his 11 into Bobby and pick that fresh "anal cherry", or so it'd seemed.

They'd gotten to his bed and ripped each other's clothes off in no time. Fletcher applied some lubrication on his already hungry shaft with some oil that had been kept in the room there and poured some into Bobby's butt crack. He then stroked his stiffness up to thrice and lined it up with Bobby's tiny, little, and obviously virgin butt hole. Knowing that Fletcher was going to enter his "back door", Bobby had then begun breathing intensely, inaudibly too, so hard as he'd then felt the tip of Fletcher's erection touch his butt.

He slowly pushed at Bobby's back hole, and Bobby's butt had then winced and winked in quick succession; it seemingly pinched the tip of Fletcher's hungry erection, and he easily realized within himself that Bobby was so much "tighter" than he'd ever imagined. It was Fletcher's first time penetrating a virgin butt hole. Even in all of that sexual tension and intensity, Fletcher had still been concerned about how he would get in without getting to hurt Bobby in any way. He cared about Bobby that much now. He tried for what seemed like a lot of minutes, pushing in, feeling just the tip pierce in, just a bit, only to be squeezed and pushed back out Bobby's butt hole when he'd reflexly closed it with his tight muscles.

Fletcher continued trying as he thought about the tight fit and squeeze; deep down, he'd wanted to penetrate Bobby. Bobby had also tried so hard not to make a fuss about it by yelling or anything; he knew he had to ease himself as much as possible. Fletcher had made visible gestures that reassured him that he was trying his best to go gentle on him and visibly asked him to remain calm. Fletcher pushed and stopped, holding the pressure of his huge erection against Bobby's virgin butt hole as he'd continuously and reflexly winked and puckered his hole, and then suddenly, Fletcher felt the tip of his 11-inch erection bore in, just a fraction, and with Bobby carefully bent there, static and no movement for some seconds, everything was still, until Fletcher tried to push in again. He heard Bobby let out a rather very faint squall and then a follow-up moan as he then transitioned into a gasp and whimpering squalling, but didn't want it to stop either.

Fletcher felt his well-oiled shaft slip a bit further with each squall and moan; he tried to calm Bobby down by quickly kissing his neck while he was at it. The full tip of his shaft had gotten in now. Fletcher only realized that it had been so tight that he almost climaxed instantly but held back! He'd wanted to really feel Bobby's tight virgin butt hole. Like some fetish patterns.

It was still only the tip of his shaft inside Bobby's butt hole, but he pushed into Bobby's warm tightness even more as he inaudibly moaned out softly. He then watched his erection slowly disappear into Bobby's tight hole; slowly, his moans began to drive Fletcher wild; even if Bobby couldn't hear them, he could tell that his noises had filled the atmosphere pleasurably enough! Fletcher couldn't help but want to hurt Bobby's little puckered, warm, virgin butt hole. He laid flat with the entire length of his hugeness inside Bobby and felt the hot, tight, finger-like suction and squeeze instantly! He was getting a different level; of pleasure from Bobby's pink-looking virgin butt hole; it was so "hot" in there as usual with any "holes" at all, but this time, very tight as well.

He's softly gestured to Bobby, asking him if he was okay so far, and he lightly nodded and smiled sharply in a very erotic stance. Fletcher then started to thrust Bobby's virgin butt slowly as he knew he'd just picked his "anal cherry", and this was new to them, and he'd found himself being emotional about it. Also, he wanted to know and feel every inch of Bobby's hole. He thrust into it slowly for a couple of minutes; Bobby's whimpers and "cries" eventually turned into moans of pleasure, right there!

Fetcher had found himself helplessly loving the feel of Bobby's insides, not bothered about anything at all at that point! It was hot, not warm; it was tight, really tight. It held on to his shaft firmly; it was a feeling he'd never felt in a very, very long time. Basically, it had felt like some finger-like organs were massaging his erection manually as he kept sliding it into Bobby. Fletcher now thrust into it a little faster and deeper, and it had Bobby shaking and biting the foam beneath him unconsciously. His butt winced around Fletcher's size, squeezing it tighter; as Fletcher scraped his "p-spot", Bobby was going to climax! He did, hard!

Fletcher kept on thrusting. Going into Bobby's little hole, now just for the sheer loving of the wonderful sensation he was getting. He continued on the same pace for another couple of minutes, then watched Bobby give a sharp "thumbs up" gesture. His shaft grew as Bobby's hole tightened around his pounding shaft. He thrust into Bobby's little tight hole, deeply as he went on, and felt his butt muscles start something that felt like a suction massage on his shaft as Bobby easily climaxed again!

Fletcher couldn't help but bury his hugeness into Bobby's tight butt hole deeply and sprayed his load deep into Bobby as he climaxed too. Bobby whined helplessly beneath him and whimpered as her multiple orgasms faded.

Fletcher laid there on the top of Bobby's soft butt cheeks, with his erection still in through the tight hole, leaking his cum inside of Bobby. His anal muscles started pushing Fletcher out even though he tried to stay, just to keep having a feel of it. He seemed to have gotten rather addicted already! And he had still been a bit hard. After a few moments, he muscled up some strength and slowly flipped his shaft out of Bobby for a clean-up session afterward. Bobby's tight butt hole had been eased up, at least a little. He hadn't had an anal orgasm before.

They moved into the bathroom together to clean each other up, and even at that point, the boys had both felt like they had wanted more of each other; they could see it in their eyes, the way they looked at each other was conspicuous enough. Another kissing session was started in the bathroom shower space there! And then hurriedly rushed out of the bathroom space and back to the bed, to probably "kill each other" this time around, or so it seemed!

On them both getting gently laid on the bed, facing each other's sides, both realizing just how much they'd really been fighting emotions towards each other, how they had both really craved for each other, more now than the last time. With Fletcher directly close to Bobby there, more empathy and mutual emotional thoughts and wills, eyes to eyes, nose to nose, he paused to catch Fletcher's gaze for a moment and smile at him lightly; Fletcher smiled back, in awe of the glare in Bobby's beautiful eyes. He leaned in to kiss Bobby again. Slowly and more passionately this time. Bobby had started to moan under his own breath. He held Fletcher tightly to himself unconsciously for a while before trying to reach out for Fletcher's then-jogger pants to pull them down.

In an entirely and sensually reflex response again, the boys then both sat up aggressively to rip each other's towels off. Fletcher, watching Bobby's exposed and aroused nipples beg for him to rain down on them, rushed in to give them a hard squeeze before using his tongue on Bobby's. Now completely eaten up by all of that happening fast, Bobby moved his body in rhythm to Fletcher's pace, more intensely this time. He moaned and groaned out as Fletcher had kept on tonguing his rather very, very sensitive, darkened nipples. He felt his erection grow between his thighs as Fletcher had kept doing his thing! He realized how much he had missed this feeling, all of that had reminded him of how Lisa had adorned his entire physicality the way Fletcher had been doing now. It instantly became clear how much he had actually needed it without even knowing. He unconsciously pushed Fletcher's head towards his erection area. Fletcher knew what he had to do!

He went down on Bobby, firstly, licking each side of his already conspicuously rather very sensitive inner thighs for a while before going on to bless Bobby's still-tender tip with his wet tongue and lips. Fletcher would then brush his lips against its opening and then flip his tongue around it in a circular motion and continue the cycle to listen to Bobby helplessly move his body and moan out in extreme ecstasy, not having any idea of how loud his moans had really been. He then moved up to Bobby's belly button area to caress his waiting torso for a moment, only to have Bobby helplessly push Fletcher's head back to his erection.

After a few moments of "eating" Bobby rather properly, Fletcher then flipped Bobby over on the bed, gave his butt cheeks a few rounds of loud, "inaudible" slaps, he then went ahead to kiss Bobby's butt cheeks and then lubricated Bobby's "hole" with more than enough saliva, enough for it to welcome his first digit into Bobby, and then two, and then three, with Bobby responding to the slightly painful pleasure in a series of rather very blissful groans as Fletcher went on. Bobby had then arched himself a little bit in Fletcher's direction, signaling Fletcher to stick his stiffness into the hole already! He was hungry for it, and he couldn't wait to take Fletcher in either. The little mistake he'd made was failing to check for Fletcher's "size" before craving for it to get stuck into him.

Bobby heaved helplessly as Fletcher slowly introduced himself into Bobby, helpless at the time. There was no stopping anything at that point either! There had been enough saliva to lubricate Bobby's entrance as they went on. Bobby heaved heavily again on the second thrust of Fletcher into him! The painful pleasure effect had now become more pronounced. Bobby could not hear how really loudly he'd been letting his moans out, but Fletcher could understand and let him express himself. Bobby's moans at that point were music to his ears. He wanted more; he was aware that Bobby wasn't having any ideas of how loud his moans had been.

When Fletcher was convinced that Bobby was "ready" to take his 11 inches, he pushed it into his "hungry hole" gently from behind. Bobby inaudibly gasped out loud in pleasure and slight pain, but the former was more conspicuous! That was the first time he'd been "penetrated", and while he couldn't describe all that had been going down in his head, he knew that he was having a great time, pleasurable moments with this guy he'd met at the ski resort, and now has come such a long way with, not asking himself any further questions why they had been doing what they had been, and just enjoyed the whole action, so far.

It felt like he hadn't been properly "cared for" this way in years. Fletcher, as always, was good with his thickness. Bobby shut his eyes tightly in pleasure as Fletcher had kept digging him from behind, and even when he would want to flip himself over, Fletcher held him back in place.

"You are not doing anything; I'm pleasing you alone today", he whispered gently into Bobby's ear.

Fletcher maintained a slow pace as he thrust into him from behind again, there on the bed. He watched Bobby's apparently "soft" butt cheeks wobble with every thrust he made.

He increased his pace gradually, only to listen to a helplessly pleasured Bobby moan out uncontrollably. He'd felt like he was in "heaven" at that point; he was "on top of the world", under Fletcher, he was being pleased beyond his explanation.

Fletcher climaxed. Pouring his load on Bobby's butt as he'd moaned out loudly in utter ecstasy. The "mutual feeling" was divine.

Motionless, Bobby laid there, still trying to get over the pleasures that Fletcher had just served him. The boys were very satisfied with each other.

After the quick bath, they lie close to each other to talk about how they'd been in their respective endeavors over the past few weeks that they'd been "away" from each other. They had obviously made up for "lost time" together, even though there seemed no "obligation" for that. He had talked about starting an official "relationship" with Bobby. He'd declined instantly. After the way, Lisa had seemingly bailed on him, and his still prevalent and strong fear for anything "commitment", it would rather be a new relationship with a Chinese man instead, other than western "douchebags" he'd had been coming across with so far.

It was bliss, everything so far, his personality, his charisma, intelligence, the personality, his family history, and all that, but Bobby decided that he was not going to rush into anything now as he'd done with Lisa, and it seemed like a good idea. They would remain just mere "loverboys and fuck mates" that pleased each other's sexual thirsts and hunger till he was ready for another level of commitment. Forgetting to worry about what Fletcher was going to do about his unwillingness.

CHAPTER SEVEN

When he'd gotten back to his place, Bobby received the texted message from Owen. Telling Bobby that his father had gone through the videos they had talked about and was rather very impressed after seeing them. Let Bobby know that his father was interested in meeting him "specially" in person. Bobby felt lucky enough to have someone of the caliber that Owen had described to him seek for his presence like that. Bobby agreed and told Owen that he would fly into New York the next week. He told Professor Fred about it. The professor was glad and mostly very happy for his "special student", although unsure how to feel about Bobby's seemingly amazing talent soon getting exploited right under his nose. He feared for that, but he was proud of Bobby nonetheless. He told his mother, Fletcher, Chris, Tricia, and every other important person in his rather small production crew group.

Bobby had explained to them that he might not be fully around for the next week and was going to meet with a "top filmmaker". They, too, were happy for Bobby, apparently taking strides in the right direction.

Fletcher celebrated with him in the "little way" that he could in the evening. He took him to a spa for some physical massaging and therapy, one he felt that Bobby had needed so much, after such terribly long and busy weeks, even without specifying. A rather very satisfied and happy Bobby was grateful to him and acknowledged that he had been busy so much that he didn't realize how much relaxation time he had missed.

The next week arrived, and Bobby was a go on Monday morning. He'd taken a direct Delta Airlines flight to JFK. And followed the directions that Owen had sent to him. Bobby got to their mansion in no time. Owen had given him the codes to the electronic gate to gain entrance as soon as he arrived. On getting in, Bobby quickly found himself in awe of the artistic images that had hung on the walls around the outside space. It was on the outskirts of Southampton, so there was noticeable, rather very beautiful greenery almost all over. The "works of art" frames he had seen all around the place left him quickly fascinated!

He called Owen's phone to let him know he had arrived. Owen had been "most pleased" to welcome Bobby. He immediately told Bobby that his dad had suggested that they both go over to London to help him handle one of his minor projects, a small TV series. And explained to Bobby that his father had already grown so much faith in him just by seeing Bobby's staged plays and was open to welcoming Bobby into the bigger world of the film industry under his tutelage.

He'd told Bobby that his father had said; if he liked what he saw with the London project, he was going to sign Bobby into his company and work together on more future outputs. And convinced Bobby that he might end up getting in control of big-budget movies even before he knew it, irrespective of the fact that he couldn't hear stuff or speak at all. Just exactly the attribute that made it all seem so special.

"Wow! All this is just too good to be true. I mean, I only started directing a few months ago, and now I'm going to London to handle a real one. I'm not really sure about how I'd fair, Owen.", Expressed in the quickly written note Bobby gave to Owen, figuring that there was no way he would have understood the real sign language gestures if he'd demonstrated all that to Owen, excited and worried at the same time.

"Awe, don't worry, Dad is a nice guy. He'd definitely show you the sticks," he texted Bobby's phone in response.

"We're going to be on it together, so even if we disappoint eventually, we do it together too," he added in a follow-up text message to Bobby.

It was a seeming dream come true for him! He had always wanted to explore beyond the borders of the Americas, taste new cultures, and see new perspectives, and he was definitely going to grace this golden opportunity. He'd let out a light smile after hearing what Owen had told him before going on to relax his head for a little breather. He had been slightly "exhausted" from the trip. Owen gave him some fruit juice and bananas to munch on while Bobby had waited for his father to arrive. A few moments later, he did.

"Wow, he's very handsome too! I must say...." Owen's father said to him.

Happy to meet Owen's father, such a huge personality, for the first time, had him fighting hard to contain his excitement, as he tucked it all in a mild smile while getting up to return the extended handshake from Owen's father.

Owen's father had then introduced himself as "Mr. Spencer" in a beautifully written note on the light-green piece of paper from the bundled bunch on the table close to him there. He acknowledged that what he had seen in the videos that Owen had shown him was an amazing one for someone who just actually started directing stuff rather very recently and could neither hear nor talk but still communicated so much creativity.

"I've always had things in my head, Sir," he wrote back happily.

"I just let them out on set, and they get to turn out the way they do", he added.

"Beautiful!" he exclaimed, then wrote it down on the piece of paper.

"Is this how he communicates? Written notes?" Mr. Spencer asked Owen in a slightly worried tone.

"No, no, he's more accessible with text messages and a personal interpreter too. Works seamlessly," Owen responded. His father concurred.

Going on to propose the actual project Owen had earlier mentioned to him and even promised to employ him immediately after his college graduation into his studios, giving him the proposed project as a "test-run" of his capabilities. He had told Bobby to put his best into it, elaborating that it grossly mattered in his "entire future" there.

Mr. Spencer explained to them, Bobby and Owen, that even though the project was a personal one of his, they should NOT take it for granted and try, as much as possible, to bring forth rather beautiful results. They concurred.

After explaining to Mr. Spencer that he would be available for the project immediately after the semester was over, Bobby penned the signature of acceptance and returned Mr. Spencer's extended handshake. The man had been more brief and direct to the point than Bobby had originally expected.

A few hours had passed, and Owen got to show Bobby the room he'd be staying in for the night.

"You wouldn't mind if I came to keep you company all night, would you? Owen "jokingly," asked I his texted message to Bobby before watching him smile and then, "jokingly", slamming the door at his face.

Bobby flew back to Ontario the next morning and headed to campus to meet up with Professor Fred and explained to him all that had gone down with Mr. Spencer. On hearing the man's name, the professor was quick to remember some of the not-so-popular movies and TV series of Mr. Spencer that he had seen in the past and explained to Bobby that he had been really lucky to have gotten to meet with someone like that. He'd then told the professor that it was made possible by his son and joked about Owen seeming to "like" him so much already.

The semester was almost over now, and the final year in college was gradually coming to an end. Chris and Ashley had now decided that they were going to get married to each other. Bobby was happy for them. They had been together almost throughout their time on campus. Bobby felt sad about the Lisa part of his life. No longer worried about her at this point, but one part of him had felt that they just might have ended up the way Chris and Ashley had if things had gone great with them, the way it was "supposed to". Even if she had come back now with planet-sized apologies, he wouldn't want to hear explanations she would want to render to him. He had completely lost all interest whatsoever. Even if she were probably dead now, knowing that she had lied to him all that while, for still unknown reasons, he would only mourn her and her memories for a few hours and then move on afterward.

Bobby had now completely "moved on" with his life; although it wasn't easy for him and rather very disappointing to him each time he thought about it, it was seemingly the best thing for him to do. Fletcher and even Tricia had been giving him all the psychological and sexual support he'd probably needed, and he was "comfortable" with it.

He had been handling his academic projects and directorial duties consecutively towards the end of the semester. And at the end of her final examinations, he had done two more plays for the arts faculty, to raving positive reception and reviews, again!

In such a little while, he had made a name for himself. Professor Fred was proud of him all the time. Bobby had been his best student for a long time now. Dazzling handsomeness, pure talent. He knew and could tell that he had a bright future ahead of him.

Their graduation ceremony was a huge compliment. Bobby's mother was there to listen to watch him make his "speech". Felt a little bit emotional about the fact that her bright son needed an interpreter to pass his message across to the ones that needed it, but it was all good, so she'd thought. Fletcher, who didn't have any family members around and didn't want any of them either, was equally proud of him. He needed very little interpretation to understand the gestures Bobby had been making in his amazing speech and couldn't get enough of it either! It was a blessing, watching him do all of that, the specialty, the privilege, not just anyone could do that, and he was proud of Bobby. One hundred percent!

Professor Fred had sat directly behind Bobby in slight awe. Bobby had been the best graduating student in the faculty. And while he had been talking so eloquently, Fletcher, though, right there, in the middle of the crowd, also fantasized about getting in-between those warn thighs of his again that night, when all of that was over. Chris and Ashley had been happy for him, too; he had always been the smartest of all of them, so him being the best of his set had come in as no surprise to anyone at all. Most of her production crew people had been in attendance too. They were pleased to see that their creative director had now proceeded into the next stage of his life. Bobby, in his rather very inaudible condition, had been a blessing to each of them, in many creative ways

Later that day, Wendy approached him calmly and carefully apologized to him for being so mean to him all the while. Bobby easily obliged to forgive her and acknowledge that all she did was now in the past and requested that she look forward to the "better" future ahead. Wendy was surprised because she didn't expect it to come down that easy. She was amazed at the maturity that Bobby had now been operating in. There was not much of anything else that she could say or do.

On the night of the ceremony day. He knew he was down for some hot sex from Fletcher. He'd had the extra keys to Fletcher's apartment and wasted no time rushing down there after he'd gotten home.

He had made sure the entire space had been in order for Fletcher to come and meet him waiting. But plans changed! Miss Sarah had been longing for "something crazy" for a rather very long time and decided that night was going to be the tipping point, threatening that their secret was going to be heard by people who shouldn't if he didn't listen to her and satisfy her "absurd cravings". Bobby knew he had to cancel all he was going to do for, and with Bobby that night, and easily thought of something that seemed "convincing" enough for Bobby to believe!

A few minutes after Bobby had started waiting, Fletcher came in and saw him sitting there, where he was, appearing rather really tensed up, with Bobby getting visibly scared immediately and asked Fletcher about whatever had happened. He told Bobby that he had just got the news about his very good friend getting involved in a deadly car crash and now fighting for her life at an ICU. Surprised and rather frightened at the same time in reflex response, panicked immediately.

"Oh my God! How'd it happen? Is she alright?" Bobby asked in a desperately texted message!

He got no response from Fletcher. Instead, he went around grabbing a few items from his bedroom in complete pretense before walking fast-paced past Bobby and stepping out the door.

What a killjoy. Bobby had been so ready to have some "fun" that night before heading back home and then to New York. He wasn't sure of the next time he was going to ever see Fletcher again at that point, and at least one sensual moment between them before he left for his new frontier, should have possibly made him feel better. But a huge opposite had happened.

Sad and worried about the said friend of Fletcher as he was, Bobby then quickly headed back to his apartment instead. Only to find out that Chris had organized a little congratulatory party for everyone in their block circle, making him one of the VIPs. Looking at the bright and cozy space he'd now found himself in and then reading the sweet words that had been written on the cards brightened his moods a bit, and he found himself feeling better immediately. Chris told him about a "bigger party" going down that night and asked him to come with them to attend it, but Bobby softly declined, he was rather going to have himself relax at his place, after such a "long day", and then, and pack up for home the next day instead.

He opened his eyes to daylight. It was time for him to head back home to his family. His mother had tried to reach him earlier, but he had been too deep in sleep to feel the vibrations from the phone right beside him. When he replied to the message from mom, she had then let him know how much she was proud of him, all over again, and how much Barry had been looking forward to seeing him again too! He explained to his mother that he would be back home in no time. He had said respective goodbyes and hugged everyone he wanted and needed to. Tricia had already left for wherever she wanted to go, so she didn't get the opportunity for them to exchange a proper "goodbye".

Chris and Ashley promised to still be there for him, irrespective of the new lives and journeys they would seemingly embark on afterward. There were warm tears as they bid goodbye and watched him leave the apartment block.

On getting back home, his brother was most happy to see him. Bobby got a bit sad noticing the huge skin dent at the right side of Barry's face, obviously due to the crash, but he was still happy to see his only brother again. His mother had been speechless most of the time as she felt utter happiness watching her little boy, now a fully grown man, take all these strides now and becoming a better person. She was pleased. And hoped that his father, wherever he was, was pleased with him too.

Bobby had then told them that he would be heading for New York as soon as the next week for the project he had on his hands and explained to his mother that it would take him overseas. Stating how much he had always wanted to go to London, and now, he had been given the opportunity on a golden platter.

She lamented about Bobby not spending at least some more time with them and pleaded with him that he should move slower a bit instead of hurrying the way he had been. Bobby wasn't going to listen to that. He wanted to head to London and start up work as soon as possible.

He reached out to Owen and let him know that he was headed to New York next week. He concurred.

CHAPTER EIGHT

After a "crazy" night with each other prior, Fletcher and Miss Sarah had still been recovering from the various rounds of orgasms and crazy thrusting positions in wild forms they'd embarked the night before. His "well-spoken" size didn't seem to make Miss Sarah flinch much the way others would have, and now, she didn't seem like she was ever going to get tired at any point. She was an aggressive nympho and felt that she had met her exact match in Fletcher. But he was completely convinced that she was his own "exact even match" and was thinking of bailing on her as well; she was the crazier one and wondered what could be done to crush that "confidence" completely.

He felt the lightbulb turn on over his head when he remembered an old friend of his that "specialized" in "crazy" and was guaranteed to calm Miss Sarah's libido like ice on candlelight. She'd been working at a nightclub in downtown Ontario Club, an "ex-girlfriend" of his had introduced him to

Molly, for her to fix Fletcher's then-young, aggressive libido and size since she couldn't even think of doing any of that with Fletcher. The sex between them was FIRE, he and Molly. He loved the sexual freedom he had with her; for the first time then, he could penetrate, suck, and lick her just the way he wanted, without fear of anyone crying about his enormous size, or getting hurt in the process.

He remembered that Sarah had always had a fantasy of being "dominated in public", but not in a place where she could be easily recognized, and Molly was her best bet, right now! She really needed to be humbled, Fletcher thought to himself sarcastically! So, he'd contacted Molly to help him set it up and have it be the main show for the said night, at least for old times' sake. But it was not going to come free! Molly also remembered how really good Fletcher's "capability" was and made sure he promised her that they were both going to have a moment too, just the both of them, behind closed doors, acknowledging that she too had missed that shooter!

All were agreed, and Miss Sarah looked forward to whatever "crazy" thing Fletcher had for her, she anticipated, but at the same time shook with some uncertainty. She had never seen Fletcher this confident about any sexual topics but was all in for it; she liked it!

They eventually got to the venue, and immediately, the floor attendant could recognize Fletcher, and then, they escorted them both into the party room. Soft music played in the background while other attendees had talked among themselves, noticeably. Some made out in the corners of the room, but none of the "couples" was going at it, the way it used to be like he'd seen in the past.

"See? The fun thing about a sex club is, you never knew what experience you would get, not even when you paid for it, right?" Miss Sarah whispered to Fletcher sarcastically.

"Well, it's no surprise at all; all you could hope for was an orgasm at the end of the night." She added confidently!

Molly had briefed the attendants that Fletcher was going to visit them with a friend of his and had told them what to do when he came with her, that "friend of his". They could never forget about Fletcher, the one who made their boss scream and cry out like some pony getting ticked the way she did, surprised everyone in the club when he feasted on Molly back then. He was still a "champ", and each of them still wanted to have a taste of this dude!

One of the floor attendants went in and then gently blindfolded Miss Sarah and tied her to a bed in the middle of the room. Miss Sarah knew where she was and then felt her confidence levels drop drastically! She was glad that this hot chic only tied her hands and her legs had free. She hadn't even seen who would "service" her and didn't want to lose all of her control. But her heart was beating out of her chest already; Miss Sarah had gotten so scared and so turned on all at the same time. Fletcher sat by at one of the rather very comfortable chairs and watched patiently, already getting highly entertained!

As she lay there, with zero visibility, she easily noticed that the music had stopped and all the talking had stopped. Smart as she had been, she could tell that the "great Molly" must have come out and shown up, and her different fantasy was about to start. Miss Sarah hadn't heard her voice or felt her touch, but the anticipation wet her insides already, and she'd then crossed her legs to relieve the tension her thoughts had already created.

"I'm Molly Summers, lovely. You may address me as Mistress. Do you understand?" were the first "cold" words whispered into Miss Sarah's left ear.

The extent of flamboyance in Molly's "controlled" voice caressed her like silk. Tremors cascaded through her body, and for the first time, Miss Sarah couldn't tell if it was fear or lust.

"Yes." A blindfolded Miss Sarah responded softly

"Yes, what?" Molly asked sharply.

"Yes, Mistress." Miss Sarah prompted!

"That will be the only pass you get. Next time, I will punish you." Molly threatened!

It was real! The slight fear. Miss Sarah doubted herself a little bit and wondered if she was really "ready" for this experience. She remembered how she always bragged to Fletcher, knowing that he was surely there somewhere, watching all that had unfolded, decided that she was going to try her very best to maintain composure!

Surely, Miss Sarah had gone through lots of sexual experiences at the clubs and all of that, but nothing like this so far. Her heart was beating triple-time at the thought of "punishment", or so it already seemed, and she couldn't tell why or explain any reasons! What did she mean by that? Miss Sarah didn't want to find out, so she kept her mouth closed and tried to go with the flow.

She had been slowly stripped off her jean pants and had most of her body already exposed.

"Awe. Did you wear this for me?" Molly asked lightly.

She ran her fingers down her belly, down towards the "V" of her legs, and back up again. Miss Sarah whimpered, longing for Molly to touch her already swollen clitoris and give her the first "release" of the night. But Molly only grazed the pit of her belly, toying with her pleasure points and putting me even more on edge.

"Yes, Mistress." Miss Sarah whispered gently, going with the whole flow!

"I like it. You're beautiful." Molly added gently

She continued to stroke Miss Sarah, never wavering from her already "established path". She tried to position her labia in line with Molly's fingers, hoping that Molly would pity her desperation and graze her already waiting sweet spot. But Molly ignored attempts and continued playing around where she wanted to. Miss Sarah had felt like it was torture to crave a stranger's touch so badly, but there she was. And Fletcher is also still watching the whole thing unfold, sheer entertainment and visual pleasures!

She stopped touching Miss Sarah, and she groaned in grief. The crowd was quiet, so Miss Sarah's displeasure had been very obvious. Though Molly didn't touch Miss Sarah, she could feel Molly's presence close to her. Standing there, probably watching her, taking in her body and planning the "attack".

"Your safe word is red," Molly said audibly.

"Ummm, why would I need a safe word?" Miss Sarah cried. A scared question that had Fletcher bursting into slightly loud laughter where he'd sat!

Miss Sarah had hoped that she didn't sound as stupid as she'd felt at that point.

"What the hell did I sign up for? A safeword? What was about to happen to me where I needed a safe word?" were questions that had kept pouring into her slightly frightened, curious mind! Indeed, this was all as crazy as it could all get already, and Molly hadn't even started with her yet! Molly patiently dealt with her, and she was going to answer in a polished and "professional tone". And she was really good, Molly!

"Now listen, love. Although my focus will be to give you pleasure like you've never felt before, sometimes it can be overwhelming. You may desire to stop, and that's my way of knowing if that time comes. It's also there for punishments, which you are about to receive, girl." Molly whispered at the back of Miss Sarah's left ear again.

Miss Sarah's heart pounded heavily in her chest. It seemed so loud; she thought for sure that the onlookers could probably see the imprint of its beats. She didn't respond for fear of getting herself in deeper water.

"What had I done?" Miss Sarah asked herself curiously.

Through her anxiety, it came to her. She forgot to call Molly "Mistress" when she'd asked about the safe word.

"Turn over onto your knees," Molly said calmly.

"Yes, Mistress." Miss Sarah replied

The straps binding her to the bed were long enough for her to cross her hands at the wrist. She "maneuvered" her body, so she was on her knees afterward. She couldn't uncross her arms, so her chest laid flush with the bed and her but was in the air, on display. She felt Molly's weight dip the bed, and her fragrance closed in. She knew Molly was approaching. Miss Sarah was "afraid" of what was about to happen, yet her heated fluids flowed uncontrollably in arousal.

Molly touched her back area first and ran her hands down Miss Sarah's spine. Molly caressed Miss Sarah's breast, stroking her nipples in her seeming "exploration" gestures. She stayed there a moment, kneading Miss Sarah's nipples between her thumb and forefinger, before softly pinching them and progressing forward. Miss Sarah was getting the definition of "crazy" already, but more "professionally" this time, it seemed what she'd actually requested from Fletcher!

It slowly stopped feeling like "punishment", and Miss Sarah's juices coated the insides of her thighs. Molly took her time, continued her exploration, and ran her hands over Miss Sarah's butt cheeks. Squeezed and rubbed them in utter admiration. Then, Miss Sarah heard it before she felt it. Her mind eventually registered the slight sting from the spanking against her left butt cheek. Then the right, then back to the left.

Fletcher kept watching as Miss Sarah moaned in apparent pain and astonishment at the same time. Finally, she spanked Miss Sarah, and she knew her butt was red with Molly's handprint already, such a tender skin she sported.

Ten slaps to each side! When Molly finished, she rubbed Miss Sarah's already "sore behind" gently, Molly's fingers touched her warm opening, and she moaned in delight. Then Molly pushed one digit into her, and then another. The pleasure was beyond what she'd expected after being "humiliated" in front of a room of people, in the dimmed lights, but she found that she was on the precipice of an orgasm.

"You did good, my little pet. I think I'll reward you for doing so well." Molly whispered again.

Her fingers moved in a consistent rhythm in and out of my wetness, and I could hardly hear her words over my moans of pleasure.

"Do you want to cum, my pet?" Molly asked Miss Sarah asked lightly

"Yes, Mistress." She said in extreme ecstasy

And she did. Miss Sarah climaxed all over Molly's fingers. The feeling was "delicious"! Miss Sarah's voice rose above the "audiences'" to scream levels, as she'd tried to contain the rapture rolling through her body, gentle and calm, yet ruthless and aggressive, Molly was to her, tied up and helpless on the bed space there. Miss Sarah almost screamed out her "safe word" as she'd now "understood" overwhelming pleasure.

Molly carefully rubbed her back area as the orgasm slowly subsided. She'd then lifted Miss Sarah and turned her over, so she laid on her back. Miss Sarah was in awe. Molly laid beside her, silently stroking her back down to earth. Then she whispered in Miss Sarah's ear;

"Do you want more?"

"Yes, Mistress." Miss Sarah replied softly. Still, all to Fletcher's entertainment and visual delight.

Molly grabbed a crop whip from the side of the bed. It was jet black with a suede handle. Miss Sarah no longer feared the "possible outcomes". She knew even if she endured a "small" amount of pain, the pleasure would be much greater; at that point, she was completely convinced; she loved it, wholly!

Molly positioned herself between Miss Sarah's legs and pushed them back until Miss Sarah's wet space was on display.

There was no mistaking the power of her orgasm as a result rained like water down her thighs. She continued to push Miss Sarah's legs back until she could go no further and Miss Sarah knew to hold them there or receive another "punishment".

Molly then laid beside Miss Sarah on the bed and ran the crop whip over her nipples, gently flicking them with the whip until they were stiff peaks refusing to stay hidden from the light.

She ran the crop whip down Miss Sarah's body, up her legs, over her feet, and between her thighs. Molly flicked her labia, and Miss Sarah jumped at the slight "sting". Molly did it again, and pleasure overcame the sting, though the sting was still there. Repeatedly, Molly tapped her until she writhed on the bed seeking the orgasm that once again had been built in her "core"!

Molly moved the crop whip, and it hit Miss Sarah directly on her already enlarged clit. The lecturer jerked in utter pleasure; the feeling she was getting from Molly was overwhelming. All atoms of fear had gone, and now it was just hunger, and more hunger for Molly, or anyone, or anything at all

The flicks on her clit increased in speed, and the moans and groans of the crowd submerged hers. The orgasm built to a painful "crescendo", and Miss Sarah "came" loud and proud once again! She couldn't control her legs as they twitched across the bed, abandoned.

Her "Mistress" held her to the bed as her orgasm continued for moments longer than she'd ever experienced. Her body was tense with released pleasure.

Miss Sarah was done. She could take no more. In between heavy breaths, she sighed,

"Red."

Her "Mistress" kissed her head and stood up from where she laid close to her.

"Are you not entertained?" Molly asked while looking at Miss Sarah in a sexually hungry gaze.

"Yes! Yes, I am, Mistress," the lecturer replied.

Molly took the blindfold off her face.

"Good, now you're gonna have to do me the same way," Molly said to Miss Sarah.

Unknowingly to her, Miss Sarah had been the slightly shy type around "strangers", in a way. She strongly felt like there was no way she could pull off her "best moves" on Molly while the others had been watching.

"Okay, Mistress, let's do this in the other room instead," Miss Sarah said with a soft voice tone, pointing at a visibly open and empty room space from across where they had been at. Spotting an aggressively smiling Fletcher beside the entrance, well sat, apparently having a great time watching her get wasted by his "recommendation".

"No, you're the mistress now; I tremble at the words that come from your tongue and the wiggles that emanate from your fingertips now," Molly said in a well-constructed response.

They moved to the other room space. It was cozier, conspicuously. The music rock hard from the club vibrated through the walls in the dim light that radiated from the chandelier at the very center. At that point, Fletcher knew he was free to have sex the way he'd wanted to; now that Miss Sarah was off his sight, he surely then went on to help himself with the lady down the counter who'd been giving him "signals" all the while!

There was a bed with red and black-colored sheets precisely in the other room where the mistresses went to.

"There's the toolbox, Mistress," Molly said to Miss Sally while pointing at an enclosed space at the far corner of the room.

"I haven't met you before, and I am so sure you'd make this coochie scream," Molly said in a more confident tone.

"You look like it, Mistress, show me something," Molly said as she slid up on the bed and slid her panties off while her leather mini skirt was still on her, then she lay there and nodded her head slowly.

Game on! Miss Sarah thought to herself as she went over to the box Molly had pointed at and found a few whips of different textures, blindfolds, brushes, spatulas, strap-on artificial penises, and a bunch of other stuff.

She pulled the box closer to the bed where Molly had stayed, waiting.

"What can I do for you, Mistress?" Molly said softly, fixing the intense gaze on Miss Sarah.

"Turn around", Miss Sarah responded, apparently about to freely unleash some "sensual mayhem" on this "unfortunate subject" as payback!

Molly then turned around as the lecturer latched on to the nape of her neck with a soft bite and then flipped her hair over to the front. Molly freed herself and completely surrendered to Miss Sarah, waiting for her imagination to descend. She let out a soft moan when Miss Sarah bit the second time.

Then she went on to grab Molly's hair aggressively, pulling her head all the way backward, exposing her bright, spotless neck before she then slowly caressed Molly, throat to chin with her tongue, and planted a kiss on her lips from behind

Molly reciprocated! Miss Sarah slowly pulled off her red-coloured bra cups.

"How do you like that?" Sarah asked bluntly in a sensual tone!

"Please me, Mistress", Molly eagerly responded.

Miss Sarah flipped her over, so Molly's rather "average-sized" bouncy breasts faced her directly. Sarah descended on them with both her hands, gave them a warm, rhythmic massage before she went on to caress the already stiffened nipples with her tongue, and extra saliva for easy lubrication!

The skin on Molly's breasts conspicuously radiated with so much glow! Miss Sarah felt her ocean filling up down there in between her legs. It appeared that Molly had easily sensed it and reached out for Sarah's honey pot with her fingers. Miss Sarah pushed her hand away.

"You are not allowed to touch the Mistress yet, girl. My rules, you keep 'em!" Sarah said afterward.

Molly obliged.

Miss Sarah then went on kissing those hard nipples of Molly for a moment still. She moaned and cried out softly in Sarah's ears; she was being "worshipped" and loved it so much!

Miss Sarah stopped, went over to the box that she had drawn closer. She opened it up to bring out a pair of plastic-feeling handcuffs, slowly tied Molly's hands in them while still looking into her eyes.

"Now, this is the last time you'd see me," Miss Sarah said to her.

"Yes, Mistress", Molly softly responded.

"Sip this ass, punish me, please", she added.

Miss Sarah took out a long piece of silky linen, turned Molly around, and placed the blindfold on her face.

The music from the club hall still pounded softly in the background.

The lecturer pulled Molly a little bit higher on the bed space there, pulled down the skirt she had been on, revealing her bare butts, her succulent, gorgeous, bouncy butt cheeks. Sarah kissed every inch of it softly, top to bottom, slapping hard as she bit some parts of it lightly. When Sarah reached Molly's labia area, she easily realized that it was filled to the brim with heated juice, waiting to be sucked dry.

Miss Sarah then pulled out the spatula from the box there and teased Molly with it, rolling it from the nape of her neck to the bottom of her butt cheeks. Molly began breathing more heavily as she let out light moans in rhythm with the rolling spatula on her body.

Miss Sarah reached out to Molly's honey pot area with her fingers and located her already erect and rather very slippery clitoral tip; her "inside" was moist and warm already, dripping with still hot juices. She flipped on Molly's clitoris tenderly with her fingers and listened to her moan as it slowly became louder.

"Shush! Don't you make a sound!" Sarah said softly to Molly's ears.

"Yes, yes, Mistress," Molly responded amid intense pleasure.

Sarah intensified flipping actions on Molly's stiffened, tender clitoris. This time Molly couldn't help but react with aggressive body movement afterward! She had then arched her back in different directions, she moved her waist in the same manner, and she couldn't help but start moaning out again; she grew rather very impressed with Miss Sarah in no time!

Sarah had found some duct tape in the "toolbox" and used it to "shut her up". She'd been moaning too loudly. Something that Fletcher might have skipped doing the last time he had been with Molly on the same bed space.

Her entire body already seemed beyond her control. Molly had appeared as though she was overly extra-sensitive as each little flip Sarah made on her clitoris had made her scream behind the duct tape in response, each flip!

Sarah had been getting really wet and "juiced up" already while she was doing all of that to this new lady who'd only punished her just a few minutes before, and now, she wanted her, or anyone else to just get her laid and hard already, this time with something as "humongous" as her standardized "Fletcher size", to fill up every inch of her already heated, wet and slippery walls.

After a few minutes of flipping on and massaging Molly's clitoris aggressively, she climaxed. Sarah could tell that it was an intense one and felt like she hadn't even started with Molly either too. Sarah's suspicion of Molly being overly sensitive had turned out to be true.

She wasn't screaming anymore, and Miss Sarah's hands weren't moving anymore. Then she pulled Molly's legs apart, moved up to her warm honey cup and started to eat her up. The moaning came back again, this time, more aggressively. Sarah moved from Molly's clitoral "hemisphere" to her warm opening and back to her clitoris, and the cycle continued.

Sarah's tongue had refused to stay still as she'd kept brushing Molly's clitoris and listened to her moan out loudly and helplessly behind the duct tape. Sarah felt "wicked" at that point; she could easily tell that Molly wanted to scream out to have a full feeling of everything.

"I'm don't think I'm a strict mistress, or am I?" Sarah thought to herself as she let Molly off the tape and went back to eating her. With Molly's hands tied, and her eyes forcefully closed, and her getting all that good stuff from Sarah's tongue, she "came" again!

Although Sarah realized she wasn't as "professional" at this as Molly obviously was, she figured satisfying Molly was probably always this easy, not knowing if that impression was a wrong one or not. It seemed like she didn't need really much of any "aggressive effort" for Molly to orgasm twice.

"What a great Mistress you are! Oh My God! More!" Molly basically cried out in ecstasy.

"Do you like how you're being treated?" Miss Sarah asked gently.

"YES," Molly responded.

"Now, we're gonna fuck each other's brains out," Sarah bluntly said to her in a very sensual tone.

Miss Sarah then brought out the "huge" strap-on dildo from the toolbox. Molly asked her to go first; she'd also asked Molly to go first!

They became "sarcastically undecided". And it lasted for a few seconds till some lady walked into the room there, where they had been on their "stuff".

She'd sported a radiating dark skin, green-tinted hairdo. Nearly petite, with her crop-top and leather skirt on. A rather very beautiful one too.

"Yo, I could hear y'all having a good time here from the other room," the lady said in a blunt, rather erotic tone.

"Is there some space for one more? I want in." The lady added.

"Sure, there was room for one more". Sarah basically thought to herself. She was there to have the most fun and "enjoy" herself that night, thanks to Fletcher's "bright idea" So, definitely, there was room for one more.

Molly then politely asked Miss Sarah to take off the blindfolds so she'd be able to see who was making the "request". She was "hot" enough, apparently. Molly did not hesitate to request that Miss Sarah took off her bindings and have them "engage" her, perhaps in ways she hadn't "experienced" before, as punishment for interrupting their "sacred moment".

"You want in, huh? You wanna feel good too, right?" Molly asked her softly.

"Well, what do we call you then?" Molly continued.

"Green, call me that," The lady responded.

"Okay, Green, let's fuck!" Molly said.

Molly was unusually straight and direct to her. Miss Sarah then calmly told Molly that they ought to "engage" her, Green, together. So she realizes the people she had come to "mess with", or something like that, sarcastically.

They were both "horny" and wanted some pleasing, Molly and Miss Sarah, but first, the urge to please Green seemed paramount to them too. Both "Mistresses" had seemed like hungry vampires waiting to drink up the blood of their prey. But in this scenario, heated sexual fluids.

They moved over to Green slowly and began undressing. As calm as they were. She had been on a white-looking sexy crop-top and a dark-colored leather skirt. Miss Sarah and Molly made sure all that came off nice and easy—revealing Green's bare breasts and darkened nipples.

Green was a "hot girl", obviously enough, and she had been slightly bushy down there. Miss Sarah had always loved "bushes", a fetish of hers. That turned her on, struck a nerve in her head.

Molly started to kiss Green from her neck, and Molly went on to her thighs and behind her knees.

Both "Mistresses" brought her down to the bed there in the room. It remained as cozy as it got, with the sounds of music from the club hall still vibrating softly through the walls.

Molly placed Green's hands behind her back and tied them up with the hard piece of silk linen that Miss Sarah had used on her.

Sarah slapped Green's butt hard and listened to her moan out in response. She'd cried out and requested that Sarah should hit even harder, as hard as she could! Miss Sarah had rather very tender palms, so she'd figured that it might not make any difference from what Green had been getting because she had been hitting Green really hard all the while. Sarah then took the plastic spatula and then slapped Green's butt cheeks with it,

"Yaaaas! That's the spot, baby, do me like that," she said in extreme ecstasy.

Miss Sarah then went on hitting both sides of Green's butt as she moaned out in response to each "hard slap" from the spatula she had received.

"Now you see us, now you don't," Molly said to Green softly before picking another silky piece of cloth to cover her eyes. Molly moved in for the kill.

She kissed Green's neck and bit hard on her shoulders; Miss Sarah went down on Green's breasts and bit hard on her nipples. All Green could do was nothing but scream hard as they went in on her. The intensity continued. By this time, Molly had kissed every inch of her upper body, and I had sucked the life off her nipples.

"I want someone up my ass", Green screamed as she panted heavily.

"Oh, not yet, Good things take time, love", Molly said to her in response.

Miss Sarah went down on her. Green's honey pot was as "delicious" as anyone could imagine. Dug and buried her head right there in the middle, in-between Green's legs.

With Sarah effortlessly sipping her "hot juice" and chewing softly on her hard clitoris, Green moaned uncontrollably. Molly was still all over Green's breasts and neck; she switched to Green's butts and spine area, using her tongue to brush and bless the various pleasure spots found on Green's "hot body".

The mistresses could tell that Green was out of the world already, and unfortunately for her, she couldn't move a muscle. Miss Sarah kissed, nibbled, bit, and sucked on her warm honey pot; Sarah loved it so much that she barely noticed Green's shaking legs until a few moments later when she was about to have her orgasm.

And when it came, it was a milky one! She'd ejaculated her hot, heavy load all over Sarah's face. And she let out a scream of relief after that.

"Oh damn! I'm in heaven! Oh Lord, is that you?" Green cried in complete ecstasy!

Molly went on to use the duct tape on Green to close up her mouth again and prevent her from making any sounds.

"You scream too loudly and talk too much," Molly said to Green sarcastically.

She reached out for the strap-on dildo they had left there on the bed. It was a dark-colored, "humongous" one.

Molly went on to strap it on her waist, and before Green would know it, she had suddenly been taking the rather "huge load" from behind.

Green had kept on screaming behind the tape on her mouth while Sarah was on her nipples again.

"She could channel all that rage to something more useful", Miss Sarah thought to herself. So she took off the tape from Green's mouth and fed her with "honey pot" fluids instead. Instantly, Sarah realized that Green was that good, even in the "bondage", she made the lecturer scream her brains out.

The hard rock music had still been playing from the club hall behind them. The room had felt a bit warmer now. There were three ladies aggressively doing their thing. Moans resonating in-between the walls, extreme pleasure all over the atmosphere. Molly was penetrating hard and deeply into Green. From behind there, with her legs and hands tied up, and her eyes shut, and her mouth and tongue forced to bless Miss Sarah's "space" with all its capable goodness, she could only oblige to the situation she had found herself in.

She was now moving back and forth, in perfect sync with Moly's multiple penetrations from behind her. Molly went from slow to aggressive, and slow again, to aggressive. Switching paces the way it suited her. Each time she went faster, Green would "eat" Sarah more aggressively. Miss Sarah would feel the force of Green's wet tongue grace the surface of her stiffened clitoris and drove her crazy.

With Molly behind a tied-up Green, there was no way Miss Sarah could get any of them to squeeze her breasts for me. The lecturer was on fire, so hot that she had to tingle her nipples all by herself and aggressively squeezed her breasts as Green kept on digging her tongue deeper within Miss Sarah and then resulted in another orgasm. This time stronger than anyone Miss Sarah had felt that night. Something about the way Green had "eaten" her drove her nuts in a rather very "different way".

Molly probably decided that she was done with Green for the time being. She pulled Miss Sarah over to where she was, placed a warm kiss on her lips, pulled Sarah's leg up to her waistline, went under, and reached out for Sarah's labia again.

The lecturer had just recovered from one orgasm, and she was probably about to go for another one. She'd lost count of how many she had seen or felt that night.

Green had still been breathing heavily and couldn't say a word. Molly and Miss Sarah had gone beyond the "Mistress" methods this time, and it seemed like all rules were dropped, and we both wanted to really "open up to each other".

They kissed each other again, this time more aggressively. She pushed Miss Sarah to the bed; Miss Sarah landed right beside Green. Molly quickly spread the lecturer's legs apart and penetrated her with the dildo.

"That thing is really huge", the lecturer thought to herself as she soon came crying out in immense pleasure spasms afterward.

Molly went hard; she was aggressive; this time, she wasn't in control; she was all over the place with her body. It felt like listening to Miss Sarah moan was a direct driving force to whatever she was doing, or she had just plainly loved it, Miss Sarah never knew. She could feel the dildo gracing every inch of my honey pot, from top to bottom, Molly was hitting non-stop for a moment before reaching out to Sarah's breasts and erect nipples to bless them with her tongue again.

Green had seemed to have recovered from that intensity and didn't seem disturbed with her blindfolds on when her breathing had returned to normal. She appeared comfortable for a while before making sounds that felt like "somebody, get this tape off my mouth". Molly concurred. She stopped the aggression on Miss Sarah and took off the tape from Green's mouth and the blindfold from her eyes.

Green looked at Molly and then looked at Miss Sarah before screaming, "Oh my fucking goodness!" in a short burst of excitement.

"Untie me and lemme have that dildo," Green said to Molly. She concurred.

Green put on the dildo more quickly than expected. Aggressively flipped Molly over to where she had stayed. Made her lie on her belly and asked Miss Sarah to tie Molly's hands up. She did.

Green spread Molly's legs apart and went into her with the dildo from behind. Fast-paced at first, then some slow, rhythmic paces afterward. She'd arched her waist in different angles as she'd kept on "digging" Molly to her satisfaction.

She'd then went on to flip Molly sideways and lay beside her, "penetrating" her from behind. More aggressively this time. Miss Sarah moved over to the front and shut her up with kisses on her lips, chicks, and neck. Miss Sarah could easily tell that Molly wanted to grab one of them while doing all that to her. Unfortunately for her, she could not move the hands that were tied behind her.

Green didn't stop. It felt like some form of "payback" for all the aggression Molly had rained on her previously. It was, actually. She went in harder and faster, from different angles. Molly could not keep her calm anymore. She let out hefty screams with each thrust, and it went on till she had her orgasm.

"Hell yeah, how do you want some of that!?" Green said to her sarcastically!

Molly probably did not hear when Green said any of that either. She had still been recovering from the helplessly intense pounding and enormous orgasm. She couldn't move much either. She seemed exhausted. Miss Sarah felt really exhausted too.

Green didn't show any of that. Perhaps because she had come late to the "party", or had the least number of orgasms. But then, it seemed like a great night for everyone! They quickly got acquainted in a few moments after the "bondage marathon". Green was first to leave the room afterward. Molly and Miss Sarah would go on to agree and fix a "date" for another round of intense pleasures from each other.

"Wow, and I don't even know your name." Molly had asked lightly.

"It's Sarah, Thanks! I gotta go now; I had an amazing time," The lecturer responded!

"Don't forget, same place, same time next week!" Molly replied confidently and excitedly!

"Yep, you got it!" Miss Sarah responded as she slowly got back into the clothes she'd been on. Her libido was relaxed now, and as Fletcher had earlier predicted, was now calm as cold ice on candlelight.

On getting back into the main hall they'd come in from, she'd easily spotted Fletcher sinking his erection into Green and was surprised that she could still take such a pounding, even with Fletcher's size! Slightly angered that Fletcher had gone sexual with "someone else" right before her presence, Miss Sarah stepped into the mix, pulled him by the waist, out of Green, and forced him to get dressed, and dragged him out of the club hall, back to the car they came with and drove them back to his apartment. Fletcher couldn't tell if he was in a huge mess or if it all was just "one of those things".

CHAPTER NINE

When Bobby had eventually arrived in New York the following week, it was immediately down to business. He had been briefed by Owen that his father's company was going to take care of all his expenses and that all he had really needed to do was to deliver. Bobby was to direct the first three episodes of the drama series.

He had been given a few weeks to go through the already written and revised screenplay, and he and Owen were to leave for England by the weekend.

It was the first time Bobby would be visiting Europe, supposedly for "business". But he knew that he would go for his own "pleasures" too. He told Fletcher about it, and Fletcher had ensured that he would get back to Switzerland as soon as possible to meet with some family folks of his and then come to stay with Bobby in England, if possible!

The weekend had come sooner than it felt like, and the boys, Bobby and Owen, were to head for London by Friday morning.

They'd boarded A British Airways 747 business class. Bobby did not want to sit beside Owen for "personal reasons" but stay "close to him", so he opted for a seat in-between them instead. He smiled at himself when he realized that his immediate seat partner on the over 10-hour journey was a grandma, probably in her 70s or thereabout, looking old but not tired at all. "Hello ma'am," he'd gestured to her calmly, nicely signifying that he wasn't a "talker" as he moved in to sit, with Owen behind her. "Oh, hello, kiddo," she happily responded with a bright smile on her face, but Bobby wasn't aware. He knew there was no way Owen would be able to "act stupid" with grandma in-between them. So he had felt more relaxed that there won't be much talking on such a long journey; he was wrong.

The person almost directly beside Owen was as talkative as it got! After he'd eventually come to his seat space, Owen gave way for him to move in and relax as he sat and looked at Owen with some "precision" unknowingly,

"Hey, I'm Jared," The person said, smiling.

"Owen!" he said, smiling back, unusually!

Jared outstretched his arm, extending a handshake gesture. Bobby saw all of it and was "happy" for Owen that he wouldn't get bored to death after all.

"Oh, very, pleased to meet you here, Owen", the person added eloquently.

Owen shook his head gently as a seemingly warm response as well.

"So, headed home too, I guess? You don't look like you're from around here," Jared asked gently, attempting warm sarcasm.

"Oh, not really, Sir. I got a huge lot to do over at London, so, yeah," Owen replied, not knowing how to properly interject.

Jared seemed like he was the most handsome smile freak at the time. He would always smile like some invisible person was tickling him from behind. Owen thought of him as a really happy person already, or just very jovial, even though it seemed awkward all the while. And when he would catch Bobby's gaze, the "mockery" he got from Bobby was visibly conspicuous. But Bobby had refused to laugh out.

In Owen's mind, Jared was an "okay" one, or so he thought, as Jared always had something to ask about or say before they had even departed the Ontario airport. Owen was now rest assured that Jared had been the extremely talkative type of guy, but stories he told as they went on remained entertaining to his ears all the way! Not much of a bad thing, he'd thought.

Jared told Owen how his wine production business had him travelling all over the world in specific "missions" to find the "true spirit" in his wine taste. Jared happened to be the founder and CEO of a not-so-famous or demanding wine brand. This was interesting to know because he shared beautiful ideas that intrigued Owen's philosophy in general, and Owen tried so hard to cover up for how impressed he was. Jared did the talking ninety percent of the time in any conversation they'd had throughout that flight time. Owen funnily found himself nodding to everything the new guy said all the while until he pointed out how he barely even knew Owen and found himself telling Owen so much already. That was as "awkward" as it had gotten.

"Hello stranger," He said Owen sarcastically,

"Story of your life too, if you don't mind," he added—this time, with a funnily silly smirk on his face. Feeling slightly embarrassed, Owen let out a short smile coupled with a mild apology for his seeming insensitivity.

"It's alright, I talk too much," he jokingly pointed to. Though Owen did not feel like it, an awkward will to at least say something to Jared kept creeping in. Jokingly, Owen told him he would get to know all there is in the "great story of his life" and that he'd needed to catch some sleep. Jared was a bit calmed by that and was able to shut up already.

"Hm, I could work with that, Sir," he said calmly as he laid back to relax on the headrest of the seat and grabbed a magazine from the chair pocket in front of him.

Bobby had fallen asleep already. Owen, who'd possibly thought he was going to have an amazing travel experience, found himself stuck with a "talking maniac" and then sleeping periodically all through the flight. Bobby was asleep almost throughout the entire flight, except when he needed to eat or take a pee or check up on the cute grandma beside him.

After all the hours that felt like a few moments to Bobby, obviously, they were notified of the approach to the airport, they landed at Heathrow. As the plane taxied to the docks, the atmosphere out the window instantly looked really different from what he was used to. They were in London, thousands of miles away from "home", he thought to himself. Finally, the plane stopped, and they were allowed to alight.

"First time in London?" Owen asked him mockingly and sarcastically in the texted message.

"Isn't it obvious?" Bobby had replied bluntly with a bright smirk.

He quickly noticed the hazy skies, the different spelling patterns, all that seemed like the norm there. They made their way across the airport into a penthouse owned by Owen's father's company. He was to take the night and the next day off to adapt to London and ease off any forms of jetlag before "getting to work".

Getting to the penthouse, Bobby was shown a different bedroom to stay in. Owen knew he wasn't really "comfortable" with him still, so he opted to pick a room far away from Bobby instead to give him as much privacy as possible.

Owen asked Bobby if he would like to meet a friend of his that he'd been talking to about him. Also, an aspiring filmmaker like him; letting Bobby understand that the "friend" was looking forward to meeting him in person. And now that he was there, in London, it would be nice for them to "meet up". Bobby concurred, stating that he would want to meet up with the "whoever" the next day. Bobby settled in eventually and had English "fast food" for dinner before falling asleep that evening.

Bobby opened his eyes to daylight the next morning. It was his first dawn in London. And the view through his window was a rather very beautiful one.

Owen knocked on his door to greet and told Bobby in the texted message that he'd been heading out for a stroll and asked him if he was interested. Of course, Bobby was. He had been on plain undies all night; he quickly cleaned up his face and hair and went to meet with Owen.

They had been taking a short walk down the neighborhood, and Bobby had sharply noticed the rather very beautiful and different architecture from what he had been used to over at the Canadian hemisphere. Bobby had come along with his camera, and when they had gotten back, he realized that he couldn't stop himself from taking dozens of photographs.

Booby showed some to Owen. Owen was instantly amazed at how this dude had shot them and decided to frame some of them for himself! So much creativity. He told Owen that he would like to see the guy he had earlier talked about the previous evening. Elaborating that it had to be before he went full gear on his father's project. So Owen agreed that he was going to make him available by the evening.

The friend had told Owen to come to a restaurant where he'd be waiting for them patiently at 7 pm. After a rather boring day between both of them, Bobby and Owen. They get down, preparing to go see this "friend" guy. When they got to the place, Owen instantly spotted the friend and took them there, to where he'd sat.

Bobby seemed absolutely delighted to get to meet him personally. He was average height, fantastically handsome, way more manly-looking than Owen could ever be, and the soft bright green in his eyes captured Bobby's interests immediately.

"Oh, there you are..." the friend said to them in his thick British accent, but Bobby had no idea of it; he couldn't.

Bobby had stood there in front of him, just in sheer awe of how "beautiful" this guy actually was. And the fragrance of his perfume was a rather very intense one, captivating! Remained that way for a few seconds before being able to snap back to reality when he felt his phone vibrate. He checked, and it was a message from Owen, asking if he was okay!

"Yes, I am", Bobby responded.

"Well, at least have your seat", Owen replied gently.

Owen noticed the way Bobby had looked at the new guy, and could immediately tell that there was some drooling going on.

"I'm Liam." Said the text that Bobby received on his phone from a strange number. It was from the "friend guy".

"I've been told so much about you by my friend here, and after looking at your stuff and content, I wanted to get to meet you in person." He added enthusiastically in the follow-up text.

They had a brief, quiet texted conversation there, whenever they wanted to talk, Liam and Bobby. And then audibly spoke to Owen when he wanted to communicate with him. It was a short "meeting". Liam had explained that an "urgency" had come in, and he needed to be there as soon as possible, promising them that he was going to create time for them to have a more proper "get together" eventually. The boys concurred, but also collected information and location details about the new project of theirs, acknowledged that he could be of "some help".

They got back to the penthouse, and Owen constantly teased how noticeable it was to "everyone" that Bobby had been "head-over-heels" toward Liam.

"Well, he's single too, and also gay, as well. I guess I wasn't good enough." Owen teased sarcastically.

The next day came, and Bobby was going to carry out production procedures on set with Owen. On getting there, he was instantly in search of Liam. His "new friend" had been nowhere to be found for a long while. Was he going to be late? Was he going to not even show up at all? Did he take the statement seriously? Bobby asked himself as his gaze wandered about on set for at least a sight of Liam again.

After a few hours on set, meeting with other crew members and fraternizing with all that he needed to with the conspicuous hurdle between them, his inability to speak, gotten out of the way, it seemed to be all hands on go, ready for work. Owen was there, in supervision too, to make sure everything had been going as "planned". He effortlessly noticed Bobby's strange coldness almost throughout the entire time they had been there. He had no idea why; even Bobby himself couldn't tell why he'd been so off all the while, but none of that was stopping anyone from doing all that they had to do. They wrapped up for the day, and Owen told Bobby just exactly what he had been asked. He obliged. And they left for the penthouse afterward.

A week had gone by, and Bobby was now fully ready for production duties. They had notified Owen's father about the resumption of duties, and he excitedly gave the go-ahead. Liam had shown up on set before them. Owen had given him the location details, and everyone was happy to see him again. This time, less officially-looking. He had been on a plain baseball hat and his facial hair so well-oiled, it seemed like each strand reflected sunlight. He was also on a plain T-shirt and a pair of jean shorts with sneakers. He was "hot" as ever.

He went over to Bobby and Owen to give them light handshakes, stating that he was excited to see them again.

"Brilliant! Now let's watch you lads work!" he said to Owen happily before watching them go on to their respective duties.

The work for the day was a success. Bobby, as usual, exerted so much control and creativity, and everyone was pleased.

Fletcher would always try to reach out to Bobby whenever he too could, but it quickly appeared to both of them that they had gotten so busy with their lives that they hardly ever checked on each other the way they had been supposed to! And apparently, they were getting rather very used to it as well!

Fletcher and Miss Sarah were still on their "sexual duties" alone, and Molly hadn't been disappointing either! So, Fletcher slowly became one without any viable purpose and didn't seem to care too much about it either! His generational wealth and Monarch family ties meant he really never had to work for anything. He wasn't in contact with his mom, father, or anyone in his not-too-distant past.

Miss Sarah eventually realized that he was quite the wealthy one and then decided to use all of that to her advantage as well. She had no plans for her former student whatsoever, but at the same time, maintained her aggressively territorial behavior toward him! She never let any female folk come in the picture, in between them. And Fletcher was powerless against that!

More and more weeks had passed, and Bobby was able to manage "work and play" rather very well. But he had to stay concentrated on the job, no matter what, and he knew it! Many attracted male and female folks had approached him for "something more than friendship," and Bobby being who he was, had a slightly difficult time keeping all that in check and now losing any focus.

Nonetheless, he had been dishing out top-notch results at work, and top-notch professionalism, always asking himself where all of it was coming for with the relatively very little training and experience he'd only had. In no time, Liam became too "obsessed" with how good he had been at work, and how good he had been in handling this new, pressured social life, and a slow, steady rise in fame and general recognition, and also already loved his general personality so bad that he'd bluntly told Bobby that he was interested in taking things "up a notch" between the both of them, maybe start a life together, professionally and personally too, going places in the entertainment industry, not at all showing any signs of worry over what Bobby was going to feel or think about it! But Bobby felt like he hadn't been ready for any of that yet, even if it "seemed" like a "good offer," he felt as though he needed to get his "path" right first, before ever thinking of "settling down" at all. She instantly shot down the idea and declined the request.

After such "good times," he'd had watching Bobby do his thing, Liam realized that their relationship would be better if it had just been strictly professional, for the time being. And he knew he had to kill the "emotions" he felt towards Bobby, even if it had been eating him up from the inside for a while too.

At that point, Bobby just wanted to explore his own life instead. Liam realized that the sad way. Liam requested that they'd stopped keeping any "close contact" with each other while they were still there. Although Bobby had slightly felt bad about it, he never liked losing "good people's" relationships because of his personal reasons. Bobby had no other choice than to oblige. And then tagged everybody "the same"; not being able to really see things from his perspectives and understand him properly. Back to "square one" on his personal social life, so it seemed.

The project eventually aired to warm reception all over London, and Bobby quickly grew to "great levels" of popularity and fame that he detested so much! Newspapers and editorials were filled with headlines of how a deaf dude from the west had been the mastermind behind the beauty of what they'd been given; the TV newscasters themselves had been even more sweet-mouthed, as the paradigm had conspicuously fascinated everyone! And when the news and reviews got to Owen's father's notice, he realized the true value of the investment he was making and acknowledged the bright future in front of Bobby and what it could mean to his company as well!

Bobby communicated to Owen and his father about being open to another job or project away from London there. And that he needed to be ready to travel again, over there with Owen by the next month. He was already down for it and couldn't wait! He was rather very excited when he'd been eventually told that the continuation of the series would be filmed and produced in Australia.

Bobby realized he hadn't been keeping in contact with his mother and decided to reach out to her and tell her about the whole progress too. Which his mother was pleased to hear about. He had been given the screenplay by Owen and made to understand that filming was to start as soon as he was done with digesting the screenplay. Bobby had then "innocently," asked Liam if he would be interested in coming over with him, just for the "comfort" sakes of it all. Liam sharply declined, stating he'd learned all that he needed to, and he was okay with Bobby leaving. He confessed about being sad that they didn't end up the way he wanted them to. Bobby had deeply felt hurt for him too, and he couldn't understand why either, but he wasn't heeding to any requests either. He had made up his mind already!

A few weeks had passed, and then it was time for him and Owen to move over to Australia to continue with filming and production duties as discussed. It was a rather very long journey, from London to Sydney. Two stops. It was less awkward between them this time; Owen knew his place and didn't get to show any interest in "flirting around" with Bobby or anyone at all. Any discussions they'd had were only pertaining to the project ahead of them. After almost a full day of travel time, they finally arrived in Sydney. It was the first time Bobby had been there. But this time, he had subconsciously decided that it was strictly for business and not any forms of "pleasure" or mingling with anyone at all.

They settle in another apartment in Sydney owned by

Owen's father's company. They resumed work on the series by the weekend. Bobby noticed that things like the spelling patterns and even fashion senses of folks there were the same. Rather very conspicuously! The Australians had a generally different entertainment and procedure philosophy, so they had seemed more difficult to work with because of this, especially with a guy who couldn't speak or hear anything at all. In the end, everyone managed to get the hang of it.

Bobby's time in Australia was quite snappy and more "focused" than social in any way. All work, and no play. After a little over two months, filming had wrapped up in Australia. Post-production was on now, he was to leave it for the company to handle, and she got the notification from Owen's father that the final portions of the series were going to be filmed in Florida. And he was to leave for America with Owen immediately. Bobby was stunned. He didn't want to return to the west anytime soon, he still wanted to stay away from there for a long while, to finally get the chance to experience Australia, personal touring without much ado, but sadly enough, it didn't seem quite as possible anymore. But he knew he had to answer duty calls, regardless.

By the end of the weekend, he and Owen had arrived in Florida. According to his father, it was the final part of the jigsaw. Almost a year had passed now, and he was "stable enough" to get his mom the dream car she had always wanted, and paid upfront for the rest of Barry's school bills, and even got his apartment, so he didn't always have to stay with Owen, avoiding any forms of unspoken discomfort. Even though they both had made efforts to "blend well" with each other, it just wasn't working. And they both couldn't tell why either, he and Owen.

After digesting the final drafts of the screenplay, Bobby carried on with filming as soon as possible. They would always finish up filming way earlier than scheduled. Owen, still maintaining his post as production manager was always stunned at his effortless capability and talent; he always was. Her crew management was always fantastic and left him wondering where he'd learned that from.

Fletcher, on the other hand, had been more outgoing now. Communication with Bobby had seemed conspicuously weakened, and he pretended to understand why. But secretly, he'd felt the disconnect already. And it had felt like there was nothing he could do about it either.

On his "breaks from the lecturer" and "free days" from any of the "drama," he'd always visited the Royal Ontario Museum. He was always fascinated by the sheer beauty and wonder of pieces that had been exhibited there. But, this time, on this particular visit session, he got fascinated by... someone.

"Quite the world-changer, he was," said a man behind him with one of the most masculine tones he'd ever heard in his life while he had been staring at a portrait of Leonardo da Vinci. When Fletcher had turned to look at who'd said it, he caught the gaze of a tall, dark, well built, full-bearded, rather very handsome man in a black dress shirt, black jean pants, and black well-polished suede Chelsea Boots on his feet. Fletcher was startled, fascinated, and stunned at the same time; he shivered a little and quickly tried to compose himself before the man could have noticed.

"Oh, Yes, yes, he was." Fletcher said to the "stranger" as he quickly got back his "cognition."

"He was one of a kind, I respect him and the legacy he left behind," The man told Fletcher confidently with his arms behind his back.

He had quite the slight African-American accent with him. He had a charisma so strong. And intelligence so pronounced, Fletcher, who for the first time in his life felt "small" and "submissive," had nodded to everything the man had said right there.

"Come, come, let me show you some more," he pleaded lightly. Surprised, Fletcher paused for a moment to properly catch what had been going on and then try to organize himself, and then obliged.

They walked up the escalators into another chamber, apparently very rich in other historical heritage. The man had kept on talking about the legacy of what da Vinci had left behind, his history, probably political and socio-cultural influence, as he pointed to images and items tied to da Vinci's existence in the space. He seemed to know a lot about Leonardo, so much that he'd summarized his entire life story before Fletcher realized they had completely circled the entire museum. Out of the blue, one man comes and then fascinates him that way. Granted, he was really amazed and in awe with his knowledge of just that man alone, and from the way he had been talking, one could easily tell that he wasn't playing around with any of that those things he had seen, but Fletcher kept asking himself what had really been going on! What was it that he wanted? Had he been "spying" all along? Where did he come from? Who the hell was he? The questions kept pouring into his head.

"Wow, you seem to know a lot about just one man." Fletcher said to him while halting the long walk they'd had in a bid to affirm himself not getting allowed to be "tossed" around that way.

"Oh, you flatter me, lad. It's a passion for the history and general significance of his existence," The "stranger" said in response.

Fletcher was still unsure but was "pleased" to some extent. While seeming at unrest, he couldn't ignore the fact that his heartbeat raced a little each time their gazes met. Fletcher struggled to shake off this one. Right there where they stood, there was an awkward silence for a moment before the "badass" stranger took the chance to break it,

"I'm Kendrick," he said to Fletcher, extending his arm for a handshake.

"Fletcher, Fletch, anyone," he responded while returning the handshake gesture firmly.

"You know it's vividly clear that you're not from around here, Right?" Kendrick asked sarcastically.

Fletcher had felt quite "free" with him at that point, so he explained to Kendrick about things that had brought him there, openly enough. Kendrick found the whole and sincere explanation rather very amusing!

"Women," He muttered after letting out a short giggle.

At that point, since they had been telling "stories," he then let Fletcher in on a little detail about him; he had always been a great fan of historical art and nature. And how pleased it was for him to meet someone that was seemingly fascinated about the same thing too, Fletcher. Kendrick continued and told him about his Documentary expos and how much of a professional photographer he'd become over the past few years. A statement that sharply reminded him of Bobby. But he didn't flinch. Instead, he was instantly intrigued; he had a "fetish" for creative people. He smiled at Kendrick and made him understand how "pleased" he was to have met him. Both guys took a walk in the museum again, discussing their interests about the arts, photography, and even politics. It went on and on until he got a call from Miss Sarah, asking him to return to the house as soon as possible, warning that she didn't want to have to find out herself that he'd gone out "cheating." He had no other choice, as powerless as he portrayed himself to be around her, always "obedient."

CHAPTER TEN

B obby was at the front door, asking if he could come in, she rushed and hugged him and kissed him, and he kissed her back, and as she'd invited him into her bedroom, just so they could go on having some "fun" eventually, she quickly got up from the bed in the middle of the night. The strangest thing had happened. Tricia had seen Bobby in her dream, or "nightmare"! She was stunned; Bobby could talk! And the voice tone imagination she had of him was quite the magical one! It had never occurred that way before. She couldn't fall asleep anymore. She had stayed up until the next morning's daylight.

Tricia had missed Bobby a lot, but not to the extent of she almost having sex with him in "dreamland." She figured that it had probably been her subconscious trying to show her how much she needed to be touched by him again. It had been months since they last contacted each other, she and Bobby, and even though she could care less about what he was going to feel about it at this point, she wanted to respect him and not even bring that "topic" up anymore. But as the days slowly progressed, she couldn't stop herself from reaching out to him.

When Bobby excitedly accepted her request to see him, it felt like that was the most relieving thing she'd ever heard in a while, and by the next week, she was in Florida already. At his address that day, she had waited for a little while before Bobby was able to finish with duties that day and head back home.

When the two "beneficial friends" saw each other for the first time in months, they couldn't contain the excitement; Tricia couldn't contain her libido. Her loins signaled her immediately. Bobby rushed in for a hug. Like drifted souls who'd found themselves after decades, the two friends held on to each other longer than either of them had imagined. Then, the sexual fantasies kicked in! From hugging to caressing, right there at his door porch. Reaching out to her soft butt cheeks and massaging them lightly. Tricia's breathing got heavier! The urges were mutual!

At that point, Bobby's hormones as well had been raging already, and he could barely wait to dive into all that goodness that had been longing for him too! He unlocked the key knob, banged his door open, lifted Tricia off her feet, and then straight to his bedroom space!

Although, there had been a little bit of sheer "awkwardness" in the atmosphere between them! It was quiet, too quiet for a while, with them staring at each other for a short moment, trying to absorb the sudden intensity of all that just happened in the blink of their eyes. And then, after all of that, Bobby made the first move, leaned in for a kiss to her forehead, then a slight brush of his lips to her lower lip, and then graced her entire mouth space with a sensual lip-lock! Turned on instantly, she kissed him back, just like it was in the dream she'd had a few days earlier! That little moment between them was earth-moving! His kiss was different this time, the way he moved his lips on hers, the way he tucked his tongue into her mouth, the way it collided with hers, the feeling was different, it was divine, Bobby had "improved" exponentially! She wanted more immediately!

In no time, things got way more intense! Before they had realized what had been over them both, their clothes had begun coming off their bodies aggressively, and then, bodies were being thrown on the bed there! Completely naked as they were now, Bobby helplessly adoring all of the sexual goodness right in front of him, goes down on her and gets her warm and hungry "hole" area even more lubricated with his saliva, then takes his time slowly on her as he went on sliding his whole hand between her legs, spreading her "cheeks" as though they were bread buns waiting to be divided! Then, he flattened his fingers and began massaging all around her butt hole, too, satisfying his fantasies! A slightly shocked Tricia gasped a little before promptly asking what he had been doing! He couldn't hear what she'd been exclaiming with, but he didn't care; he wanted to "do" whatever he wanted, and she wasn't about to stop him either.

"Hush," he gestured, gently placing his index finger on her lips.

Right there, Tricia could tell that it was going to be no "ordinary" encounter; she was excited and ready for whatever this "aggressive" Bobby was about to "punish" her with. So she lay there, completely submitted, allowing him to have her all the way!

Bobby slowly continued, rubbing in circles at first, just basically teasing the crinkled center, then backing away for a moment, showing so much "experience," so it had seemed to Tricia. She groaned instantly and spread her legs apart the more, giving him "better" access. Bobby wasn't sure about how she felt toward what he had been doing to her, but he was willing; he wasn't going to stop! Although she was initially a bit uncomfortable, she knew she had to free herself even more for this "experience." Bobby teased her rear space with his middle finger still and felt it magically open up and stuck his finger in, the more! A sharp intake of breath seemingly announced just exactly how pleasured she was becoming, but she alone could "hear" how she'd been feeling.

She then pushed back a little as he inserted the second finger; she groaned in pleasure, then silently screamed, "Oh fuck, that's good, oh fuck." Under her breath, inaudible to Bobby, as his third finger slowly went in, stretching her butt hole wide, to more pleasure than any pain this time.

He looked down and could literally "see" inside her between his fingers; he twisted them back and forth and watched as saliva had kept flowing all over the space between her legs! He eases his hand out, and she looks around in a slightly disappointed expression that suggests she wanted more! He headed over where there had coincidentally been some Aloe Vera gel on the closet furniture there, to be "used on him," and then he gestures;

"Now, it's your turn."

Unwinding completely, she then gives off a "devil face" grin and reaches for his throbbing erection, going on lubricating its entire length with the aloe vera gel he'd handed to her and then reaching back and squeezing his soft testicle sac. She then turns him around, pushes him over the carefully polished wooden table in the space, and repeats what he did to her—stroking his butt hole too, building up to three of her smaller fingers while jerking his already erect shaft aggressively at the same time. Surprised that he didn't seem to flinch much, she then agreed within herself that it definitely wasn't his "first time" either! Bobby groans in helpless response, trying to concentrate and keep himself from "climaxing" soon! It had felt so good, the way she was doing it, like some "pro" of sorts.

She let out her primal instincts on Bobby, and it seemed like they had been guiding her "properly." She'd slowly withdrawn her fingers and realized just how really messed up it had all been so far; she pulled him into the bathroom space as they rinsed each other afterward while still stroking and caressing their "units" all the while. Bobby turns off the water and steamer and grabs his white towels, drying her off while still in the warmth of the shower space.

They then slowly stepped out of the bathroom space, and Bobby sat her down on the rather dapper-looking makeup seat in his bedroom space, and started to slowly lotion her body with one of his body lotions, smoothening the "cream" on her pretty looking butt buns, while starting at her feet, how he'd missed all that! Bobby had conspicuously been in utter admiration of every inch of her at this point, just like old times, and couldn't wait to dive into her eventually! Tricia takes deep breaths of pleasure and comfort, with her eyes closed, enjoying the sensation she was getting from the massage.

He then leads her to the bed again and pushes her face-down on the cover, grabbing a pillow and putting it under her hips, thus elevating her bouncy butt cheeks! He found himself getting lost for a moment, having to stand back and admire the view for a while!

"Oh man, what a body.", Bobby secretly thought to himself.

He then leaned over, and pulled her butt cheeks apart slowly, and looked at her perfect little pink-crinkled rosebud. He instantly imagined what and how it would feel like again when his erection would slide into that hole, one more time, how it would probably be getting massaged tightly, but his gentle nature always ensures he took things slowly! Her labia opened up, and he could easily see her juicy center, small, tidy "lips," and the pearl of her stiffened clitoris; he could recognize it all; everything was still the same, as "beautiful" as it got. Wetness and feminine energy still oozing out and trickling down to the pillow. He lowers his head and scoops it all up, running his tongue over her clitoris, through her wet and slippery opening, and up to her butt area, centering the tip on her hole. She starts to let out unfortunately inaudible animalistic howls as he'd speared his tongue as deeply into her bowel entrance as it could go! It seemed to Tricia that Bobby was obsessed with butt stuff, she wasn't wrong, and she didn't have a problem with that either!

She humped back at his face, grunting and moaning aggressively, making incoherent noises as he went on; it felt a bit sad to hear that Bobby couldn't enjoy the sensual sounds of her aggressive moans. He buries his face between her glorious "globes," penetrating her butt seemingly for all he was worth. He backs away and rolls her over, lifting her feet to his shoulders and then spreading her wide. Her "honey pot" kept pouring hot juice, and he jammed his face into it, sticking his nose into her gash, rubbing juice all over, putting his whole mouth over her honey pot, and sucking. Beatrix starts thrashing around, her feet beating a tattoo on his back, her hands pulling on his hair, apparently trying to get her deeper inside. She starts to scream inaudible words as her body starts to "convulse."

Bobby had never seen an orgasm like that in a while. She twists and turns, clamping his head between her thighs. He could barely get any breaths into his lungs as she pulled on his hair and her feet thumping on his back. Her steamy "creampie" became visible all over the pillow and dripped into her butt hole in no time! Bobby then gets his erect shaft and slowly shoves it into her warm honey pot. Not being able to listen to a conspicuously amazed Tricia moan out in what seemed like a painfully pleasurable outburst because of his conspicuous thick size was the only "pain" he'd deeply felt at the time, but there was nothing he could do about it.

Her warm "cream" all over the place, she now wanting even more of that huge shaft, she found herself moving to the rhythms of his thrusts into her warmth, with it all hastily becoming more of a memorable and extremely enjoyable experience for them as they went on there. She loved what she was feeling; he loved what he was feeling. The feeling of his erection's tip scraping through the tight and slippery walls of her essence blew his mind and had him inaudibly moaning beyond his control.

A few more moments of aggressive thrusts had Bobby coming to orgasm! In turn, spilling his warm load on her bouncy butt cheeks to his utmost sensual delight! And the two helplessly watched themselves sleep off in their erotic mess afterward!

Bobby woke up to daylight the next day, and he couldn't find any signs of his partner in his bedroom space! He dashed out to the rest of the apartment space, looking for her, and making sounds out of concern, if she was going to respond at all, but she had been nowhere to be found, apparently, and there was nothing he could do about it.

And when he'd gotten to his phone to place a text message, he saw hers first, and it said;

"I don't wanna fall in love, Bobby. I'm sorry".

Bobby wondered what the reason behind that message was going to be; he was worried about her and what she felt about him generally. He dashed out to clear his head a little bit! He didn't know how or what to respond with.

He thought that; maybe, working out by jogging around the neighborhood for a while before having breakfast and heading out to see Owen for the day was going to make him feel at least a little better. It did. He'd found it easier to concentrate eventually than early that day.

When he'd gotten to Owen's, they had a "short meeting" and concluded with a common agreement on what to do next. It was a brief one because Bobby had come up with a solution rather sooner than he had expected. Typical.

When Fletcher had headed back to his apartment, while trying not to alert a quietly sleeping Miss Sarah in any way at all, he quickly remembered Kendrick had also handed his card while they were at it. He wanted to call Kendrick immediately, but then it occurred to him that even if he'd ever wanted to start something with this guy, because that was conspicuously what it was, although he hoped that he was right in his judgment on that, he might just have been moving too "fast." So, he "held back" until he couldn't anymore. Finally, Fletcher picked up the card and dialed the mobile number that had been inscribed on it. Kendrick picked up, and hearing his voice over the phone was almost instantly satisfying for Fletcher at that point, surprisingly. He found himself explaining to Kendrick how great it was to have met him in the "circumstance" that day and asked when he could see Kendrick again. He explained to Bobby how he always visited the museum almost twice a week and educated people and tourists on the history exhibited there. And said he would be available there the next day. His voice was so reassuring, Fletcher was tripping, and he couldn't explain why but didn't want to stop. He had never seen so much vigor, handsomeness, similar knowledge levels and interests, charisma in a single individual asides Bobby. At the same time, he was mind-blowing excited that he would see him again soonest; it was "enjoyable." He was in "awe," and it slightly scared him too.

If this was going to be the start of another "beautiful story," Fletcher had really hoped that he hadn't been moving too fast. He could tell within himself that he already "liked" this Kendrick guy, and he knew he needed to control himself. But strangely to him, he was seemly obsessed already, and he seemingly couldn't help it. Miss Sarah was still there; he was still open to welcoming Bobby again if he'd decided to "come back."

"Try to slow down, Man!" he constantly said to himself.

The next day, in the early hours, he sneaked out of Miss Sarah's "grips." He got to the museum building. He walked into the museum center and called Kendrick's phone; it had rung without him picking it up. Fletcher tried again, to no avail. While dialing for the third time, he suddenly heard Kendrick's soft, deep voice right behind him, where he had stood.

"Hey, Fletcher," He said calmly; Fletcher jerked a bit in surprise.

"Gosh, do you always sneak up on people like that"? Fletcher exclaimed sarcastically, conspicuously startled, feeling "bitchy".

He smiled and told "scaredy-cat" Fletcher how it was his "thing" to always surprise people. Fletcher smiled mildly and went on, walked with him.

"So, what brings you here twice a week, man?" Fletcher asked inquisitively.

He explained to Fletcher that he'd been conducting historical studies on cultural heritages in that museum for a while now and how he was almost wrapping up. Fletcher told him a bit of his own "awkward" reasons for being there, too, sparked up never-ending conversations as they walked around the museum multiple times; unknowingly to them, they had spent all the hours more than they both had originally planned to spend.

He then realized that he'd needed to get back to Miss Sarah afterward before she could begin smelling anything "fishy." He softly told Kendrick he'd be needing to leave immediately and would be looking forward to "spending time" with him again. And quickly found his way out of the building and then back to his apartment. Surprisingly enough, Miss Sarah had still been snoring in her bed. Relieved, he went over to the kitchen space to make breakfast.

They had quickly gone from strangers to really tight buddies in a little over two days. He didn't know what to think, but felt safe enough. Although Miss Sarah was, by no means, meant to find out!

The next few weeks were busy ones for Bobby. But, on the plus side, filming perfectly was now a breeze for him; his talent and professionalism showed themselves conspicuously in everything he did and everything he suggested.

The previous ones she handled were very successful and enjoyable for their respective audiences. Bobby knew he wasn't supposed to slack back; instead, keep impressing with more "amazing" content. Owen's father was particularly proud of his son and Bobby for jobs well-handled so far. Even while he was in Florida there, he was becoming popular. Once in a while, unwanted press personnel stormed his residence for interviews and all of that media propaganda. Still, his personality didn't let him give in. He'd always snubbed them and pressed charges for invasion of privacy most times.

CHAPTER ELEVEN

A few months after they got married, Fletcher seemingly became a "different person." Very different from what she had known him to be in all the months that they had been together. The sex wasn't as good as it used to be, the romance wasn't as intense as she probably thought it would become, she had wondered what had gone wrong. Even while he headed out to work and she does the same, she didn't seem to find it easy for her all the while. Miss Sarah felt as though she had made a mistake tieing the knot with Fletcher.

A few months after the birth of their daughter, Alice, he told her that he was supposedly going over to California on a "business summit" and would be out for weeks, leaving her alone with Alice. Sarah had always seen herself as "strong," so she didn't flinch about it. But, she'd hired a PI to tail him throughout his trip.

She discovered that he hadn't been to California for a business summit like he had claimed; he was getting "carnal" some men and two women as well, just for sport, all six of them. She wondered if he didn't, at least think about their daughter, if not for anything else. It broke her emotionally. She confronted him when he returned; he completely denied it and threatened to leave the house until she showed him photo evidence to his followed submission.

She cried out to him, thinking that she had found the perfect person for herself; his actions had her thinking she had been wrong all along. She promptly decided to have her way and move out of the house with Alice. He stood there powerless after all the evidence of his terrible action had been shown to him. He pleaded to her continuously, but she appeared dumb to anything he was ever going to say at the time. She was conspicuously disappointed. And decided she was going to have her revenge to satisfy herself, psychologically. Now that they had been married, all she'd really needed from her husband now was complete love and respect, and she wasn't getting it; he had broken their marriage vows.

Sarah moved some of her stuff to another "secret" apartment close by to stay away from him for a while and took Alice to be with her mother, Alice's grandma, for the week. She reached out to an old friend of hers, Jacoby, who had been residing in Jacksonville at the time. She knew how much he had always wanted to have a "feel" of her in the past, and now, being driven by the will for revenge was going to give him that chance. He was the best and most "viable" candidate for adultery. And the distance wasn't any form of a stumbling block either. Fletcher had screwed up, big time, and he was going to face the "consequence," apparently.

They had been in contact all the while too, but nothing "sensual" or out of the ordinary. He had even been invited to the wedding but declined because he couldn't watch another man grab the one he cherished so much! Jacoby was that oversensitive.

She had said to Jacoby that she was only coming to visit him for some "catching up" talk, confessing that she hadn't been a great friend for a very long time now, and she was willing to make it up at the time. He excitedly invited her over. She decided she was going to give him a rather good sex time! Her subconscious hadn't been satisfied until she had gotten her "revenge."

She got to his apartment after a long flight from Ontario. She got to his place, the described address, feared that she would get it wrong, she didn't. The door was left open; he had been on just his underpants and used his blanket to wrap his waist area when she came in. She relaxed in. Jacoby, not knowing that he had let in a horny, angry, and revenge-thirsty lady of an old friend into his space, apologized for having her see him that way.

And just when he had almost completed his statement, she briskly walked over to where he was standing and hushed him with her index finger. A gesture he hadn't expected or could have ever imagined! A wild one! That was the first time he'd been seeing her in months, and she didn't even wait for him to at least welcome her with a hug.

"How do you feel when I do this?" Sarah said as she gently pulled the tied blanket off his waist and groped his flaccid "shaft."

"Aren't you married again, Sarah? He said to her gently as he stood there in shock for a while.

"Do you like it?" she asked bluntly.

"Yeah! Sure I do, you want some of it?" he briskly responded, without thinking twice about what was happening. He had always had a craving for her since the day they'd met; back in the college days now; it was being served to him on a golden platter. He was not going to say "no."

"Sex me, Jac, sex me, please." She said to him softly.

Jacoby didn't seem to wonder why she had appeared to be so desperate. He'd already gotten his libido activated after she had groped him earlier.

He asked her to lie on the couch behind her, swiftly took off her skirt and panties. And immediately went in to taste her labia lips the way he had always imagined and wanted to!

Jacoby initially didn't want to get any more sensual with her or try to engage in any form of foreplay; he just wanted to feel her juices already. But, it was about damn time; he thought to himself as he went down into her. Licked the tip of her clitoris gently there, and Sarah let out a light moan immediately before he paused to lick his lips and digest the taste of her properly.

"Oh, do that again," Sarah muttered softly,

The pleasure from that touch sent shockwaves down her spine; it was noticeable to Jacoby. He felt good enough listening to her moan out like that. He originally wanted to just use his fingers in her, then his mouth, and then his erection, but he then found himself reaching out for her breasts. They had still been in the bra cups. Sarah leaned in for him to grab them, and he did. And slowly massaged them to her seeming amazing satisfaction. She moaned out loud and uncontrollably till she noticed a nude young, red-haired lady walk out of a room and to where they had been staying.

Startled, she stopped Jacoby to show her to him. She appeared to be unsurprised while seeing them.

"Oh, she spent the night here; she was supposed to leave this evening; I'm so sorry," he awkwardly said to Sarah.

"Come join us, love; it's gonna be fun," he sharply said to the other lady.

She was another friend of Jacoby; they'd had sex the previous night. She seemed like a bisexual personality too. She had been hearing Sarah's loud moans and came out to see who it was. She definitely knew Jacoby had been "eating up" someone already, and Grace's moans turned her on where she was.

Sarah, still dumbfounded about all that was happening, not knowing just how to respond to all of that yet, watched this other woman come closer, kiss Owen, and want to go down on her. Sarah quickly objected with a firm sit-up gesture. She had seen that particular act as a "taboo" now and wasn't ready to go forth with the plan. Molly's and Green's type of experiences were only in her past now, or so she thought.

Jacoby quickly notices it and assures Sarah that she was going to love it. She had never seen this part of him so, she constantly gave off "fish-out-of-water" behaviors while they were there. But, after a while of Owen's psychological persuasion, she finally found herself obliged to give it a "try" again. He introduced the other lady as Nina, and asked her to ease herself up and "enjoy the fun," as though it was her first time.

After the awkward "brief talk," she could see Nina get off the couch she had gone to sit on and slowly coming towards where they stayed again. She had well-shaped breasts that looked as succulent as whatever Jacoby could imagine. Sarah wanted him all to herself, but at this point, there had been nothing else she could do; her libido had still been raging, and she still needed her revenge, nonetheless.

He had only wanted to do a "quickie" with Sarah and get back to his "stuff," but now, he realized he needed to have more "fun" and get blessed by the two "meals" in front of him. He moved in on Sarah's breasts, then had his warm tongue on her now stone-hard nipples; Nina got to her in no time and shoved her hands between Sarah's inner thighs, slowly sliding her fingers all over down there! Nina placed her fingers in between Sarah's labia lips and massaged the entrance of her honey pot. Sarah was seemingly more relaxed about it than she would've imagined. While Jacoby was still in on her breasts, she then felt Nina's tongue on her clitoris; she let out a moan, as Nina dug deeper into her honey pot, she felt Nina sliding her soft tongue all over her labia area, even though she was initially uncomfortable with it, she could easily tell that Nina's "head game" was really good. She was now drowning in pleasures unexplainable as Nina kept on digging.

With Jacoby on her breasts, he asked for Nina to come up where he stayed, so he went down; they swapped duties on

Sarah. Sarah still wasn't sure of what to think about that, but it felt good! She looked into Nina's eyes as she slowly approached her face and rubbed her tongue against Sarah's lower lip before biting it lightly.

Then, Nina let her tongue on the roof of Sarah's mouth, and while now getting the hang of it and the pleasing sensations, she grabbed Nina's tongue with her lips as they deeply kissed each other, now passionately, primal nature effortlessly revealed itself. Went easier than Nina had imagined. While getting "finger worked" by Jacoby, she couldn't help but moan lightly under Nina's kisses and breast massages. Now extremely "turned on" and exhibiting primal lust, Sarah grabbed Nina's butt hard and placed her labia lips on the side of one of her legs. And let Nina stroke her body as she slid her other "lips" on Sarah's legs continuously. She was still moaning from Nina, grabbing her by the breasts when she felt the object slowly slide into her! Although Jacoby's erection was "okay enough" for her, it wasn't still compared to her husband's; it could never be! But revenge meant she kept going for the pleasures anyways. Jacoby's was more on the long side than girthy; she'd felt the load all over her abdomen. He went slowly on her while she found herself tightening her "inner" muscles to grab his stick harder,

"Yeah, do you like that baby?" she asked while listening to his uncontrollable moans.

"I live for this shit," he said as his thrusting pace became harder.

With Nina in front of her, Jacoby bent Sarah over to penetrate her from behind. She now had access to Nina's whole labia space. She tried so hard to fight the urge to descend on Nina's labia with her lips, but she failed miserably, she gave in to her lustful urges uncontrollably as she laid down her tongue on Nina's clitoris, and licked it all over, side to side, top to bottom and thrust a finger in her already slippery space, at the same time. She went rough on her, rather uncontrollably.

They got down, moaning aggressively as they kept on going; Jacoby kept hitting his old, married friend from behind, she kept on finger pushing Nina as she held on to her breasts hard. They were having a great "threesome," something Sarah hadn't expected at all but was having the best sexual moment of her life since she'd gotten married to Fletcher.

Jacoby's pace increased, and he started to moan more loudly and aggressively; Sarah and Nina knew he was going to have an orgasm soon. Nina forced his erection out of Sarah's honey pot and stuck it in her mouth as she vigorously stroked his long shaft and listened to him moan with pleasure, continuously! She placed her finger on Sarah's clitoris, nibbling it aggressively. And Sarah, in turn, reached out for Nina's and waved her fingers at the tips of her clitoris too. They moaned and cried out loud in utter ecstasy.

"Oh, Oh, Oh God," Jacoby had screamed before spraying his heated sexual fluids on Nina's face. Sarah had still been vigorously shaking to the pleasures from the intense muscle contractions in her pelvic area. She, too, had had an intense orgasm. And came back to her senses.

"You two have chemistry," Nina teased after the act.

"She's a good old friend of mine, love; she knows how to serve too," Jacoby responded to her sarcastically while keeping a surfside gaze at Sarah.

Sarah immediately started to feel some form of remorse. She wasn't the type to do what she had just done anymore; the birth of Alice had changed her completely. But she was driven mainly by the will to have her revenge against Fletcher. She quickly took a shower, got dressed, and left Jacoby's without saying anything to either of them. She took the next flight back to her state, end got back to her "temporary apartment."

On getting there, she noticed a handwritten note that said;

"Meet me at Norman's, 7:30; I have a surprise for you...."

It was her husband; he had asked her to come to a nearby restaurant so properly apologize to her for his unfortunate "wrongdoings." And she knew it; she wanted to see how and hear what he had to say for sure. Although she was a bit surprised and curious about how he'd known that she was there, the place had supposed to be beyond his reach, for the most part, but she was wrong.

She reluctantly obliged and got there earlier. No matter what, Fletcher was always too early in their "dates" as well. A culture he still kept. She spotted him and quickly realized it was the same restaurant they'd had their first "official date" in. she grew slightly delighted immediately.

She went over to where he had seated, and took out a chair for herself.

"You have my attention; I'm listening," she bluntly said.

He went on to plead for her forgiveness and explained to her that what she had seen in those videos had been a set-up from his coworkers. They told her they had drugged him with aphrodisiacs and made him want to have them, thus causing whatever she had seen in her PI's photos and videos.

Even though it all seemed like a fabricated "cover-up" to her, acknowledging that she wasn't buying any of those "stories" yet until he properly convinced her that what he'd said had been a complete truth!

"Darling, you know how much I love you; I married you to prove it; we have a kid together; if that means nothing to you, it means a lot to me!" She dished out, disappointed in him and herself as well; she wasn't the "saint" anymore; the result of her quest for revenge still had Sarah beating herself up.

"We made promises to be better people, Fletcher, and You broke that! I was broken," Sarah added

Fletcher ran out of "options"; he had to spill the "truth" to her eventually! He'd told her that he went over to see some old friends; Bobby, Kendrick, and other names he didn't think were necessary.

"Honey, the boys had missed each other a bit, and we'd thought a little get-together wasn't going to be a bad idea," he assured!

He acknowledged that they had been planning to meet up with each other for a very long time, and then, they did eventually, gracing the entire excitement of each others' presence, and for old times' sakes as well, mostly. He acknowledged that he was excited to meet them again, especially Bobby! Making her understand how he rose to where he was now, the famous deaf director, now a "major power" at Hollywood. Also granting him the opportunity for connections to more steady wealth, since he didn't meet his own "wealthy" family for anything at all – something Sarah had always confronted him about countlessly, but to no fruition – And stated that there had been "viable prospects," And then whatever happened, happened.

Furious as she was, she headed out of the restaurant and ignored him completely while he'd been screaming for her to come back. At that point, she'd had enough of his "bullshit," and there was no going back, for real!

Sarah relocated to a place far away from where Fletcher or any other person in his family would ever get to find out about! And took Alice with her and kept on warning him to stay away from them! She knew his mother might have wanted to go legal against her, but even Fletcher knew how much of a "screw up' he'd really been, even in his marriage to her. He let her punish him that way and also probably needed some time for "moral restoration" as well.

Sarah eventually moved to her new secret place, quite far away from the "world," alone, with her beautiful toddler, Alice, and grandma. As comfortable and emotionally "secure" as it got for her.

She was always awed by the evening sky in her new space, just outside her balcony, where she got views of the far horizon, uninterruptedly! Even though a part of her wasn't still deeply happy with herself and her rather very frustrating emotional life lately, she now always paid attention to the other "beautiful things" the earth had to offer, trying different perspectives on her personality to find happiness. Sarah was now always keen on listening to the birds sing out in the mornings and the noise from the water flowing by right beside the back of their building. There was hardly any strong broadband service coverage on that side of the premises, but it was all she'd wanted to. She'd still had thousands of dollars in savings, so looking for a new job, there hadn't been any forms of urgency either.

The peace and quiet, the entire serenity, gave her a huge chance to clear her head, more than she would regularly have access to whenever she was back at the city center! And it was all she wanted at this point; inner peace!

Each time, she moved to look outside, the beauty she discovered; nature. Right there, as the sun set slowly, she thought about how life had been when she was still really in love with Fletcher! When all she could think of was him, how she'd wanted to end up with him so fast, and then, ending up with such a disappointment instead! Through the beautiful evening sky, nostalgia looked into her eyes and the dim sunlight that graced her new space!

She'd gotten a new school for Alice, and when the little girl had always asked after her father, she'd tell her h hadn't returned from the said "business trip" yet!

It had been weeks now since the incident, and even while she thought that she was going to recover as quickly as possible, she was wrong, very wrong! He had felt like the complete piece to her life's puzzle! She had been building her life all around him for so long, only for her to discover such a secret after they had promised each other to be faithful and respect one another.

Still staring at the evening sky, as it slowly drifted into pure darkness that evening, she conspicuously lost in thoughts of Fletcher still! Even up till that point, she hadn't completely gotten over him; even though she lived to pretend that everything was fine, she'd always realize that everything wasn't completely fine yet, whenever she was alone, she started to "hallucinate"! Regularly testing herself, alone, most times, on purpose, to see if she wasn't going to get down thinking about anything that had happened over the past weeks, and for the umpteenth time, she'd failed miserably!

Sarah would always find herself thinking about how sweet his eyes were, how amazing his voice had sounded, how really great the sex between them always seemed like, how much of the world he'd meant to her, and all of that. She always wished that she could get so angry with him and let that anger and hate fill her up so she'd let go of him easily. She always realized that it was all easier said than done.

She had no "real friends" and couldn't trust anyone anymore at times like these. She became a loner and had only her rather nonchalant old mom to ever talk to, and the rest of her siblings were like the former her too, crazy, nonchalant, and always horny. They had all been nymphos, and she'd now hoped that it wasn't a trait that would be passed down to Alice in the end!

Fletcher couldn't change much of who he'd become now; the levels of irresponsibility were alarming. His mother tried to talk him into coming back to his "senses" but failed miserably, countless times at it. His father hadn't spoken to him in years, and he wasn't going to do that right now either, so his mother's pleas for him to do something about their "wayward" son had fallen on "deaf ears." All he cared about now was sex with the boys and anyone who wanted to have some "fun"!

Bobby, on the other hand, had become a success! All that focus, attention, perseverance, and hard work, irrespective of the odds, had paid off eventually! His disorder didn't seem like a "stumbling" block at all and always left people who knew him wondering what it all could have been like if he had been "fine."

His mother had been the proudest individual in his life! He could never hear anything she said to him out of her immense excitement. Still, he could conspicuously tell that she had been the happiest person on the planet each time he told her about every successful project there at Hollywood!

Tricia had always come in to say hello, and get "served" from time to time. Once a while, answering to Fletcher's request for sensual moments between them, just because he'd enjoyed it with Fletcher, he'd never said no! and even after his wife had caught them once already, and the initial feeling of remorse being strongly present, he'd still gone back to penetrating Bobby and Kendrick, and vice versa!

His presence in the entertainment industry in general slowly became more pronounced! His "ability in disability" became a cultural topic of conversation in almost every suburb of California and beyond! Because of him, Owen's father saw shares and media interest in his company soar beyond any expected heights so quickly!

Bobby was asked to mentor upcoming people with medical conditions like him into achieving what he had, which he accepted easily! He'd seen it as a way to "give back to the society, and jumped into the offer immediately! He loved to see people take strides against the odd. He loved his story being played out in front of him by others "upcoming individuals."

Tricia had been showing him signs of settling down soon too, but he didn't know if he was ready, but he was willing to give it a shot. Besides, who else was it going to be? Everyone who had come close to him now had all been as a result of his fame and popularity, even before his personality. But Tricia, he had a history with.

On their first "official date," a festival of texts was the order of the night, and she had also found happiness while becoming better at her sign language game until they had both gotten a shocker that no one could fathom.

The lady who walked into the restaurant, who stood shocked while they had tried to process what had been going on, was Lisa.